How much more can Michael take?

Michael's legs were shaking from the strain. He just needed to rest his legs for one second, then he'd squat right back into Naihanchi position. He quickly stood up and shook out his legs.

"Is there a problem, Michael?" Sensei asked.

Guiltily, Michael sank back down into Naihanchi. "Arigato, Sensei!" he shouted. His legs immediately started to quiver again.

"Are you tired, Michael?" Sensei asked quietly.

"No, Sensei!" Michael lied.

"Good," Sensei said. "Because you're a brown belt now. Very high-ranking student. Brown belts can't rest or come up, because they must set a strong example for lower-ranking students."

"Arigato, Sensei!" shouted Michael and some of the other students. Michael felt totally humiliated.

"And your legs couldn't have been too tired," Sensei went on. "When your body fails, you fall down. When your mind fails, you stand up."

"Arigato, Sensei!" Michael screamed again. So this was what it was like to be a brown belt? Michael felt like crying.

KARATE CLUB
Out of Control

CARIN GREENBERG BAKER

PUFFIN BOOKS

PUFFIN BOOKS
Published by the Penguin Group
Penguin Books USA Inc., 375 Hudson Street, New York, New York 10014, U.S.A.
Penguin Books Ltd, 27 Wrights Lane, London W8 5TZ, England
Penguin Books Australia Ltd, Ringwood, Victoria, Australia
Penguin Books Canada Ltd, 10 Alcorn Avenue, Toronto, Ontario, Canada M4V 3B2
Penguin Books (N.Z.) Ltd, 182–190 Wairau Road, Auckland 10, New Zealand

Penguin Books Ltd, Registered Offices: Harmondsworth, Middlesex, England

First published in the United States of America by Puffin Books,
a division of Penguin Books USA Inc. 1992

3 5 7 9 10 8 6 4 2

LIBRARY OF CONGRESS CATALOGING-IN-PUBLICATION DATA
Baker, Carin Greenberg.
Out of control / by Carin Greenberg Baker.
p.   cm.—(Puffin high flyer) (Karate Club: #5)
Summary: Will the pressure of being a rookie brown belt, sparring
against increased competition, and handling all of the details for
his parents' anniversary party prove to be too much for Michael?
ISBN 0-14-036264-9
[1. Karate—Fiction.   2. Family life—Fiction.]   I. Title.
II. Series.   III. Series: Baker, Carin Greenberg. Karate Club: #5.
PZ7.B169440u 1992   [Fic]—dc20   92-19941

Printed in the United States of America
Set in Bookman

For Chuck, Alyse, and Baby D.

Knowing others is wisdom;
knowing yourself is enlightenment.
—Lao-Tzu

Chapter One

"And I'm telling *you* the new first officer is a *spy*," Jeremy Jenkins insisted. His freckled face was almost as red as his carroty hair as he stared fiercely at Kevin Whittaker. The two boys stood nose to nose in the Midvale Middle School lunchroom.

"And I'm telling you he's *not*," Kevin shot back with a scowl. Kevin, like Jeremy, was eleven years old and in sixth grade. Kevin had curly brown hair and green eyes. "Johnson graduated first in his class from Starship Academy! He's from the peaceful planet of Siberius, for crying out loud! Captain Toltan checked his records on the show last week."

"What are you, stupid?" Jeremy exclaimed, banging his lunch tray down on a table. "Johnson faked his records. Johnson's not even human! He's a Rixian android, and a *spy!*"

Kevin raised a fist above his head, threateningly. "Is not!" he cried.

"Is too!" Jeremy shouted, raising his right arm above his head.

Michael Jenkins, Jeremy's older brother, had been watching this argument from a few yards away, trying to mind his own business. *Galaxy Voyagers* was Jeremy's favorite TV show. And, as with most things, Jeremy tended to get pretty emotional about it. But this argument was getting out of hand. Michael hurried forward. He couldn't let these two hotheads go any further. Someone might get hurt or in trouble. Or both.

For one thing, Mr. Rosario, the lunchroom monitor, watched over the place like a hawk. For another, Jeremy's right arm made a dangerous weapon. That was because right now it was encased in a heavy plaster cast.

Jeremy, a green belt in karate, had been trying to impress Sensei Davis. *Sensei* was Japanese for teacher, and Sensei Davis owned the *dojo,* or karate school, where Jeremy, Michael, and their brother Lee were all students. Jeremy had tried to break a stack of boards, hoping that Sensei would give him permission to test for a higher rank. Too bad the only thing Jeremy succeeded in breaking was the fifth metacarpal bone in his right hand, the one between the pinkie knuckle and the wrist.

What Jeremy hadn't realized until too late was that it wouldn't have mattered whether he broke the boards or not. Breaking boards had nothing to do with being ready for promotion. It was much more important to have good technique, discipline, and self-control. Lack of self-control had always been Jeremy's biggest problem. That, and a tendency to act without thinking.

"You are such an idiot, Whittaker!" Jeremy shouted, waving his right arm like a plaster club. "You don't know anything about *Galaxy Voyagers*. *I've* been watching the show ever since it started, *and* I've read every single comic book, too! I know *everything* there is to know about it."

"Oh yeah?" Kevin asked. Now he raised his clenched fists into passive fighting stance, his elbows tucked in to cover his ribs, his forearms shielding his chest. Kevin, who also studied karate with the Jenkins brothers, was a white belt with one green tip. That meant he was slightly more advanced than a rank beginner.

Jeremy, too, took passive fighting stance, though

he couldn't make a fist with his right hand since his right pinkie rested on a curving metal support. "Come on," he told Kevin. "I'm ready for you."

"Okay, okay!" Michael shouted, stepping between them. "Break it up!" He had no trouble holding both of them off at the same time. Michael, thirteen, was in eighth grade and much taller than either Jeremy or Kevin. He had also recently earned his brown belt at the promotion so he was a lot stronger.

"Get out of here, Michael," Jeremy said, turning his anger on his brother. "I can fight my own battles. I don't need you."

"I'll fight both of you!" Kevin shouted, his chest pushing against the palm of Michael's hand. "I've got a green tip now. I'll take you one at a time or both together."

"One green tip. Big deal!" Jeremy goaded, pushing against Michael's other hand. "All that means is you know the first kata."

A *kata* was a choreographed sequence of blocking and attacking moves, usually practiced against an imaginary opponent. The first kata was the most basic, with down blocks—downward strikes against low kicks and punches—and punches to the chest. To earn your first green tip, you had to go before a board

4

of black-belt judges and perform the first kata as well as some other basic techniques. While Kevin had a right to be proud of his tip, he'd be no match against a green belt, or a brown belt.

"I know how to knock your block off!" Kevin cried, punching at the air since he couldn't get anywhere near Jeremy.

"Look, Kevin," Michael said, relaxing his hold a little bit. "You don't want to fight me, and you don't want to fight Jeremy, either."

"How do you know what I want?" Kevin asked gruffly, though he made no move in Jeremy's direction.

"First of all," Michael answered quietly, "you don't want to mess with me 'cause I'm much bigger than you and more advanced in karate. I'd only make you look bad in front of all these people."

Michael watched as Kevin turned to look at all the kids at nearby tables watching the lunchtime entertainment. Michael knew Kevin wouldn't want to embarrass himself in front of the entire school.

"Second," Michael continued in the same quiet voice, "let's say you managed to hit Jeremy, which is unlikely since he's a green belt and *also* more advanced than you. But even if you *did* hit him, people

5

wouldn't respect you, because Jeremy's got a cast on. People would think you're chicken for hitting someone who's already injured."

Kevin screwed up his face, but he didn't say anything.

"And the *main* thing," Michael went on, moving in for the kill, "is that you *are* getting more advanced in karate. Now that you have one green tip on your belt, you have a big responsibility. You have to show people how a true karate warrior acts. And a karate warrior never picks a fight with another person, right?"

"Karate ni sente nashi," Kevin mumbled.

"That's right," Michael said, pleased. *Karate ni sente nashi* was the first rule any karate student learned. It meant "There is no first attack in karate." Karate was only to be used in self-defense. It looked like Kevin was finally starting to understand this.

Kevin took a step back from Michael. "It's only a stupid TV show anyway," he muttered. He picked up his own lunch from a nearby table and took off.

Jeremy, too, relaxed and sat down facing his tray. "I feel so stupid," he said, as he picked up a pint of chocolate milk in his left hand and opened the carton with his teeth. In the time he'd had his cast, Jeremy had found a lot of clever ways to work around his

6

injury. "It *is* just a TV show. I can't believe I let Kevin get me so riled up about it."

Michael, pulling his lunch bag out of his knapsack, gave Jeremy a sideways look.

"Okay, okay," Jeremy said, unwrapping a straw with his left hand. "So it wasn't just Kevin's fault. I know I've got a little bit of a temper."

"A little bit?" Michael echoed, taking a swallow of juice. *"A little bit?"*

"All right, so it's a *big* temper," Jeremy admitted. He poked his straw into his chocolate milk and took a long swallow. "But I don't know what to do about it. I try to control it, but it doesn't seem to do any good. It's like there's this horrible monster in me just waiting for a chance to jump out and bite somebody's head off. Don't you ever feel that way?"

Michael chewed thoughtfully on his sandwich before he answered. He tried to remember ever feeling the way Jeremy had described. There had been the time Lee was feuding with Jason Whittaker. Michael, trying to help, had talked to Jason's sister, Suzanne. Like Michael, she'd also wanted to prevent a fight between their brothers. Jeremy had accused Michael of being a spy for the enemy, and the two of them hadn't spoken to each other for a while.

But that wasn't the same thing Jeremy was talking

7

about. Even when Michael was at his most upset, he'd never felt like hurting anybody. Come to think of it, Michael had never really even felt that angry about anything. Mr. Mellow his parents called him sometimes, and he guessed that fit.

"Not really," Michael said with a shrug.

Jeremy shook his head. "You're always so calm. You're good at calming other people down, too. I saw what you did with Kevin. You used your brain to psyche him out of fighting. I know that's what I should have done, but I get so mad I can't think straight. What's your secret? It's like you're perfect or something."

"Not!" Michael laughed. "I'm hardly perfect. And I don't have any secret. I guess I just don't get mad like other people do."

"Who's mad?" Lee Jenkins asked, approaching the table. Twelve-year-old Lee was a year younger than Michael and a year older than Jeremy. Lee was Vietnamese and had been adopted by the Jenkins family when he was five years old.

Michael remembered the night his parents had brought Lee home from an orphanage in Vietnam. Michael's dad had woken him up to meet his new brother. Michael could still see the small, sleepy boy with straight black hair and almond-shaped brown eyes. Lee still fit that description. He'd grown, of course, but his looks hadn't changed.

Lee had just earned the rank of brown belt with black tips. That meant he was one step below a black belt. Lee had been the first Jenkins brother to study karate. His interest had inspired Michael and Jeremy to take it up, too.

"Nobody's mad," Michael told Lee. "Not any-more."

"Kevin Whittaker was being his usual obnoxious self," Jeremy explained.

Lee sat down at the table. "Oh yeah?" he asked.

"Yeah," Jeremy said. "He's just lucky Michael came along or I might have lost control."

"What was his problem?" Lee asked Jeremy.

"Oh, he thinks he's such a big expert on *Galaxy Voyagers* . . . " Jeremy started to explain. As Jeremy replayed the argument, Michael popped the last of his sandwich in his mouth and ripped open his brown paper lunch bag. Having his two brothers sitting across from him was the perfect opportunity to work on a sketch he'd been planning in his mind. His parents' wedding anniversary was coming up the following week, and Michael wanted to give them a special present, a sketch of the entire family.

He already knew what the layout was going to be.

His parents were going to be sitting next to each other with the three brothers standing behind them. Naturally, Lee, Jeremy, and Michael would be wearing their *gi,* white karate uniforms. What Michael wanted to work on now was the detail of Lee and Jeremy's faces.

Michael had taken a lot of drawing classes, and people were always telling him how talented he was. Michael hoped they were telling the truth, because he wanted to be an artist when he grew up. A comic book artist. He hoped to work for his mom's company. Andrea Jenkins was editor-in-chief at Rocket Comics, a big comic book company.

Michael studied Jeremy's freckled face, his blue eyes, and his short, round nose. Then Michael began to sketch with a pencil on his lunch bag.

"What are you doing?" Jeremy asked, interrupting his story to lean across the table. He tilted his head, trying to see what Michael was drawing.

Michael turned the drawing around. "It's just a study sketch," he said. "But it's going to be a big painting when I'm done."

"Hey!" Lee exclaimed. "It's us! What's it for?"

"Mom and Dad's anniversary," Michael said. "You think they'll like it?"

Jeremy's blue eyes opened wide. "Oh yeah!" he cried. "Their anniversary! I almost forgot."

"Not almost," Lee said, stealing a french fry off Jeremy's tray. "You *did* forget. And so did I. How many years?"

"Fifteen," Michael said.

"That's a biggie," Jeremy said, shoving a handful of french fries into his mouth at the same time. "We should do something to celebrate."

"Michael's already doing something," Lee pointed out. "You and I are the ones who haven't done anything. Maybe we could bake a cake."

"That's not good enough," Jeremy said. "This is a big anniversary. It deserves a big present. Why don't we throw them a surprise party? We could invite all their friends and Grandma Kussack and Aunt Charlotte and Uncle Herb, and we could cook a ten-course dinner like at that restaurant they like to go to, and we could put up streamers and balloons all over the house—"

"Whoa, whoa." Michael tried to slow down his youngest brother. "It's nice you want to do all that for Mom and Dad, but that's an incredible amount of work. Not to mention money. How are we going to pay for all the food and decorations?"

11

"We can ask Grandma for money," Jeremy said. "And I'll bet our aunts and uncles will chip in. We wouldn't have to cook, either. Grandma will do it all. She *loves* to cook."

Michael sighed. Jeremy was good at coming up with ideas, but he wasn't as good at follow-through. "That wouldn't be fair," Michael said, taking one of Jeremy's fries. "If we're going to throw a party, we should do it all ourselves. They're *our* parents, and they've done a lot for us. It's the least we can do to pay them back."

"I'm with Michael," Lee said. "We can't expect other people to do the work for us." He reached for another of Jeremy's french fries, but Jeremy yanked his tray away.

"Hey!" Jeremy complained. "Get your own."

"Sorry," Lee said.

"Anyway," Jeremy said, grabbing the last of his fries and biting the tops off all of them, "I didn't mean we should be lazy. I just mean it's going to be a lot of work. Why shouldn't we have some help?"

"Because we're *deshi*," Michael said. *Deshi* was Japanese for karate student. "And deshi get the job done, no matter what it takes. They don't make excuses or let anything stand in their way. You know what Sensei Davis always says. *Just do it*."

"Michael's right," Lee said. "We can't expect other people to do our work for us."

"So what do you think?" Michael asked his brothers. "Should we do it?"

"I guess so," Jeremy said, looking slightly less enthusiastic than he had when he'd come up with the idea. "How much is this gonna cost?"

"I think the bigger question is—how much money do we have?" Michael said. "We only have a week to get ready for the party, so we won't have time to earn more."

"I have about twenty dollars saved up," Lee said.

Michael scratched the figure on his lunch bag. "And I've got almost thirty," he said, putting the number beneath the other one. "How 'bout you, Jeremy?"

Jeremy's brow wrinkled, and he pressed his lips together. "Hmmm," he said. "Let me think about this for a second." He reached into the pocket of his jeans and fished around for a few seconds before he came up with a pencil stub and a dirty scrap of paper. Then he started scribbling down some numbers. Michael was surprised Jeremy had to do this. Usually, Jeremy knew exactly how much money he had, down to the penny.

"What are you doing?" Michael asked.

"Hold on," Jeremy said, doing some subtraction.

Then he looked up at Michael. "Eight dollars and eighty-seven cents."

"That's all?" Lee asked. "You're usually loaded."

"Sorry," Jeremy said. "That's all I've got. So what do you think, Michael? Is it enough?"

Michael added up the numbers. "About fifty-eight dollars. It'll have to do. But we need to make a list of everything we need to buy and figure out how much everything costs. I'll take care of that. Then I'll set up a schedule for all of us so we can get everything done on time. The hard part . . ." Michael paused to shoot a look at Jeremy. "The hard part is going to be keeping this a secret from Mom and Dad."

"What are you looking at me for?" Jeremy demanded. "I'm not a blabbermouth."

Lee snorted. "Tell me another one. How 'bout the time we were at Camp Betcham and our bunk short-sheeted the counselor's bed? Your face was so red when Doug walked in he knew something was up. And then you just pipe up about not even knowing how to shortsheet a bed so he should ask somebody else. Gee, I wonder if he ever figured it out . . ."

"Or how about three years ago when you blabbed that I thought Linda Cooney was cute," Michael said. "Everywhere I went, kids made kissy noises."

"I didn't do it on purpose!" Jeremy protested.

14

"I know, I know," Michael said sarcastically. "It's like there's a monster inside of you just waiting for a chance to jump out and run off your mouth."

"I can keep a secret," Jeremy said. "I'm older now. Besides, why would I tell? Giving a surprise party was my idea in the first place."

Rrrrrrrrring! went the buzzer. Lunch was over.

"Time to go," Michael said. "Meanwhile, you guys promise not to say a word about this to anyone."

"On my honor as a deshi," Jeremy said, raising his right hand.

"Not a word," Lee said, drawing an *X* across his heart with a finger.

"Good," Michael said. "We can talk about the details tonight when we get home."

Chapter Two

"So let me see our plan for the surprise party," Lee said to Michael the next morning.

The two of them were riding the bus that ran past the Midvale Mall. Their karate school, the Midvale Karate Dojo, was located at the mall, right between Plaza Shoes and Vinnie's Pizza. Usually they rode their bikes to the dojo. They'd taken the bus today so they could buy groceries for the party right after karate class. It was easier to carry things on the bus than on a bike.

Michael reached into his backpack and pulled out the notes he'd written up the night before. "Here," he said, handing Lee a fat sheaf of papers stapled together. "Tell me what you think."

Michael tried not to feel too proud of all the work

he'd done. He'd stayed up past midnight working out all the details.

Lee's black hair fell over his eyes as he leaned over the papers. Quickly, he flipped through page after page filled with Michael's neat handwriting and columns of numbers. Finally, Lee pushed his hair out of his eyes and stared at Michael with his mouth open. "Would you mind decoding this?" he asked.

"What's to explain?" Michael asked. "I went out of my way to make it crystal clear."

"These don't look like party plans," Lee said. "They look more like directions for how to build a nuclear power plant. What is all this?"

Michael took the papers back from Lee and flipped to the first page. "These are all the foods we can serve as appetizers," he said, pointing to a list of over thirty items. "I went through all the cookbooks last night to get them."

Lee's eyes opened wide. "But we must have about fifty cookbooks! You looked through every single one?"

Michael nodded. "Remember what Sensei says. A deshi gets the job done, no matter what it takes. Besides, it was no sweat. I'm a brown belt now."

"Okay," Lee said, flipping to the next page, which

was filled with names and numbers. "What's this?"

"Main courses," Michael said, "keyed to the page number and cookbook I got it from so we can find the recipe. You know, I was thinking. Mom and Dad like Mexican food. Maybe we can make enchiladas and burritos."

"We don't know how to do that," Lee said. "The only thing I've ever cooked by myself is a hamburger, and even that didn't come out so well."

"It's all in the cookbook," Michael said. "They've got pictures and everything. I'm sure I can figure it out."

Michael took Lee through the rest of the list, which included over a hundred desserts and ten separate schedules for preparing food, depending on what they decided to cook. Michael had tried to work out each schedule fairly so that none of them had to spend more than three hours a day up until the party.

"What about karate?" Lee complained when they'd reached the last page. "I won't have time to train if we do all this."

"Think of this as part of your training," Michael counseled his brother. "Sensei always says that karate should be part of everything you do."

"I know, I know," Lee said as the bus hit a bump, causing them to bounce in their seats. "But Sensei also says we should train at least twice a week. We can't do that with your schedule."

"Tell you what," Michael said, taking back his plan and tucking it in his backpack. "Just do the best you can. I'll cover anything you can't do."

"Thanks," Lee said. "And I'll do the best I can to help."

The bus turned left into the parking lot of the Midvale Mall. The mall was a strip of eighty-seven stores, including lots of fast-food restaurants, a video arcade, and a twelve-plex movie theater. A covered sidewalk ran along the front of the stores. The mall was so long that the bus made two stops before it reached the dojo.

Michael hopped off and ran ahead of Lee. He just couldn't wait to get inside. Since so many kids had earned the rank of brown belt at the recent promotion, Sensei Davis was starting a Saturday morning brown-belt class just for kids. Usually, all the ranks studied together, from the newest white belt all the way up to brown belt with black tips, which was the highest rank a person could hold until he turned eighteen. During class, Sensei would split the deshi into separate groups so everyone could work on the kata for his or her level.

But this was different. This wasn't a class just anybody could take. This was for brown belts only. It was time to join the big leagues, and Michael was ready.

Michael reached the dojo. The words *Midvale Karate Dojo* were neatly lettered in red ink on the plate-glass window. Beneath the lettering was a red satin banner with a gold embroidered circle. Inside the circle was a clenched fist over crossed *sai,* slender pointed weapons that looked like swords.

This was the symbol for their style of karate. The gold circle represented the Ryukyu island chain in the Pacific Ocean between China and Japan. The style had originated on the island of Okinawa, which was part of this chain.

The clenched fist stood for empty, or weaponless, hands, karate's primary weapon. In Japanese, *karate* literally meant "empty (*kara*) hand (*te*)." Okinawans had developed this empty-handed fighting technique because they'd been conquered many times over their early centuries, and the conquering warlords forbade them to carry weapons.

The sai was one of the few weapons sometimes used in karate by more advanced students. Like other karate weapons, it was based on a simple farm tool the Okinawans used when they had no other way to defend themselves. Originally, the sai was a pin used to hold together the wooden yoke on a pair of oxen.

Michael pulled open the glass door of the dojo and raced into the front hall, where he quickly kicked off his sneakers. Shoes weren't allowed in the classroom. Michael stooped to pick up his sneakers and threw them into the bottom of a closet on the right wall of the hallway.

Then he ducked through the curtained doorway that led to the main classroom area, or deck. The room was large and square with a polished wooden floor. The wall to Michael's left as he entered was technically the front wall of the classroom. On it hung flags of the United States and Japan and framed black and white photographs of the *shinden,* the karate masters.

The wall across from Michael was covered with mirrors so deshi, the karate students, could watch themselves and make sure they were practicing their techniques correctly. There were two more curtained doorways in the mirrored wall. One led to the men's locker room and the other to the women's locker room.

On the right wall hung weapons like the sai. There were also *nunchuku,* two wooden sticks connected by a rope, that could be whipped around like a flail, and *bo,* long wooden rods with tapered ends, used for striking and stabbing. Now that Michael had his brown belt, he could start studying a weapon. Lee's weapon was the sai. Michael still wasn't sure which one he wanted to specialize in. He planned to try them all before he made up his mind.

Before entering the room, Michael and Lee bowed to the shinden, showing their respect for the teachers who'd come before them. Then they crossed the deck to the men's locker room, bowed again to the shinden, and went inside.

Dwight Vernon, who'd earned his brown belt the same day as Michael, was standing in front of the full-length mirror. The white sleeve of his gi was rolled up, and he was flexing his biceps, which bulged impressively. Dwight worked out with free weights, and it showed. He was a few inches shorter than Michael, but he was a lot tougher.

Like Michael, Dwight was in eighth grade. His eyes were a warm light brown, amber actually, and stood out against his dark brown skin. His black hair was cut very short.

"Lookin' good, Dwight," Michael said, crossing the cold cement floor. He grabbed a clean gi from his locker and quickly put it on.

"I do look good, don't I?" Dwight joked, striking

another pose. "Do I look like a brown belt or what?"

"What about me?" Michael asked, trying on his new brown belt and crowding the mirror next to Dwight. He struck the *yo-i* or "ready" position, his feet shoulder-width apart, his clenched fist held down in front of his thighs. He tried to make his face look very serious and warriorlike.

"Oh brother," Lee said with a laugh. "It must be nice to think you're hot stuff."

"You got it," Dwight said, wiggling his eyebrows. "Brown-belt class, here we come!"

Chapter Three

A few minutes later, Michael was warming up with the other brown belts while Sensei Davis led the class. A sturdily built man in his late thirties, Sensei Davis had straight sandy-colored hair and a droopy mustache to match. Sensei Davis was a third-degree black belt.

The eight students formed two lines, front to back, facing Sensei. Since Michael and Dwight were the two newest brown belts, they stood at the back of each line. Twelve-year-old Jamie Oscarson was the highest-ranking student in the class, so she stood at the front of the line on the left. Like Lee, she had a brown belt with black tips, but she'd earned her rank before he had. Lee, second-highest in rank, stood at the front of the second line, on the right. Behind them stood other plain brown belts who'd held their rank longer than Michael and Dwight.

"*Ichi, ni, san, shi . . .*" Sensei Davis counted in Japanese, starting with the number one. After each count, the deshi would kick up first their left legs, then their right, to stretch them. Then they did head and neck rolls, side stretches, and a few other warm-ups.

"So far, no big deal," Dwight whispered to Michael as class members jumped up and down to get their blood moving. The walls shook and the mirrors rattled as nine pairs of bare feet pounded the floor.

"It's just like any other class," Michael agreed. Maybe he'd taken this brown-belt thing too seriously. After all, a karate class was a karate class. So they'd learn a new kata and new techniques. That was exactly what they'd been doing all along.

"*Yame!*" Sensei Davis commanded them to stop. "Line up along the wall for deep knee bends. Advanced students will form line in front, new brown belts behind."

"*Arigato,* Sensei!" all the deshi shouted. *Arigato* was Japanese for thank you. One of the first and most important things Michael had learned in karate was courtesy. You said thank you all the time, after re-

25

ceiving a command, getting a correction, or working with an opponent.

Michael and Dwight raced each other to the side wall of the dojo, the one with the front hall door that faced the mirrored wall. Michael and Dwight stood side by side in yame position while the six other brown belts lined up in front of them. Following Sensei's lead, they placed their hands behind their backs and tucked their fingers into their belts. Then they all balanced on the balls of their feet, their heels lifted off the floor.

"Ichi!" Sensei counted.

Michael, Dwight, and the rest of the class dropped down to the floor, their butts resting on their heels, their knees jutting out at a forty-five degree angle. Then they popped back up to their original positions.

"Ni!" Sensei called.

Everyone dropped down and popped up again.

"San . . . shi . . ."

Deep knee bends had never been Michael's favorite exercise. They were hard on your knees, and your legs got tired. On the other hand, they really strengthened the quadriceps, the big muscles on top of your thighs. It was important to have strong legs for kicking and squatting and staying rooted into the floor. And they never did more than fifty. Michael would get through this the way he always had.

After the first set of ten, Sensei nodded to Jamie Oscarson. "Pick up the count," he said.

Jamie was medium height, her black hair pulled back into a messy braid. Her gi was worn in the knees and elbows, and her brown belt was tattered in places.

"Ichi!" Jamie called as the class dropped down. "Ni . . . san . . . shi . . . go . . . roku . . . shichi . . . hachi . . . ku . . . ju!"

Thirty more to go. Lee picked up the count next. "Ichi! Ni . . . san . . . shi . . ."

Michael's legs were beginning to ache, and he wasn't popping up quite so fast, but he tried not to let anything show in his face. He was a brown belt now. Brown belts felt no pain.

After Lee, Rosalie Davis picked up the count. Rosalie was Sensei's daughter. She'd just turned thirteen, and she was almost as muscular as Dwight. She wore her sandy hair in a ponytail that flopped up and down as she easily did the next set of ten deep knee bends. Michael's legs were starting to burn now, but he tried to look on the bright side. They only had one more set.

A brown belt named Chuck James counted out the last ten. *I can do it,* Michael coached himself, though it was getting harder and harder to rise up once his knees were bent. He remembered a quote he'd read on the bulletin board: *"Karate is ninety percent mental, ten percent physical."* Well, Michael's mind was strong, even if his legs weren't.

". . . Shichi . . . hachi . . . ku . . . ju!" Chuck finished the count.

Michael breathed a sigh of relief. He'd made it! But he'd known all along that he would.

"Pick up the count," Sensei Davis said to the next brown belt on line, Alyse Walker. Sensei's hands were still tucked behind his belt, and he was still standing with his heels raised. "Two per count."

Dwight shot Michael an alarmed look, and Michael was sure his face looked the same. How many more would they have to do? And how could they do two deep knee bends per count when their legs were already aching?

"Ichi!" shouted Alyse, a slim girl with shiny black hair. She was standing directly in front of Michael, and she seemed to have no trouble as she started the next set. Michael, on the other hand, felt as if his legs were on fire. Dwight, too, looked like he was in serious pain. Sweat was pouring down his face, turning his gi a damp gray.

Slowly, Michael dropped down then forced himself up again. Even slower, he did the second one.

"Ni!" shouted Alyse.

Michael began to feel like an old man, but he somehow got through Alyse's set. When they were done, he looked hopefully in Sensei's direction. They'd done twenty more than usual. Sensei had to give them the command to stop.

Sensei nodded to the boy on Alyse's left, a thirteen-year-old with curly dark hair named Nelson DeGracia. "Three per count," Sensei said.

Michael didn't even have the strength to look at Dwight this time. He felt like he was standing on the edge of a cliff with a stampede of wild buffalo racing toward him. The only choice he had was to jump, and there were nothing but sharp rocks below.

"Ichi!" Nelson shouted energetically, dropping down and up three times.

Michael didn't know what to do. He couldn't stop. But his legs didn't want to bend even once more. Okay, so he'd been wrong. Brown belts *did* feel pain. That was no excuse to stop, though. He had to make himself do it, or he'd look like a fool in front of everyone else. Michael tried to blank out his mind completely, to screen out the pain. And, somehow, he made it through the next set, though he was the last one to rise on the last count.

"Yame!" Sensei gave the command to stop. "Shake out your legs."

"What legs?" Dwight whispered to Michael. "I can't even feel mine anymore."

"I wish I couldn't feel mine," Michael said as he shook his right leg. Hot flames shot up and down his quadricep. His left leg felt just as bad. But Michael couldn't help smiling. This had been the toughest thing he'd ever had to do physically, and he'd made it. The rest of class would be a snap after this.

"Staying in your same positions, we'll work kata," Sensei said. "We'll start with *Naihanchi Sho,* the first brown-belt kata. New brown belts, just follow along as best you can."

Michael already knew a little about the Naihanchi kata. Unlike the white-belt or green-belt kata, which moved forward, back, diagonally, and sideways, the Naihanchi kata only moved sideways. The idea was that you were backed against a wall by several opponents, so you couldn't move backward, and your opponents were closing in on you from the front and sides.

There were other differences, too. In the white-belt and green-belt kata, your techniques were loose and quick except at the moment of impact, when you tightened up. Then you let your body relax again until the next move. In Naihanchi kata, once you finished a move, you had to keep every muscle tight and tense. This helped build up strength and endurance.

Sensei stood in front of the two lines, his back to the deshi. Michael watched Sensei's reflection in the mirror on the opposite wall so he could follow along.

"By the count, half speed," Sensei said. "Yo-i!" Sensei bowed, then hid his right fist behind his flat left palm, both hands covering his groin. "Ichi!" Sensei looked to his right and crossed his left foot over his right, so that the ball of his left foot was touching the ground. His forearms came forward to cover his chest and stomach.

Michael's legs were still burning, but he did his best to copy Sensei.

"Ni!" Sensei called. He stepped down on his left foot and swept his right foot up in front of his left knee. At the same time, he jammed his left elbow back so that his left fist was pressed against his ribs. This was called putting the fist in the pocket. His flattened right hand struck out sideways as he stomped on the floor, hard, with his right foot. The move ended in Naihanchi stance, a squatting position with the legs wide, the heels turned out, and the toes turned in.

As Michael painfully lowered himself into the Naihanchi stance, he remembered another difference between Naihanchi kata and the other kata. In Naihanchi kata, you squatted almost all the time. You never came up, except for a very few moves. Which meant that if your legs were already sore from a hundred deep knee bends, you were in big trouble.

"Now hold that position," Sensei said, rising from his own Naihanchi stance. "And hold your bodies absolutely rigid."

Taking his time, he walked toward Jamie and pressed down on her extended right arm. Jamie's right arm didn't give at all because she was holding it so tight. Then Sensei walked toward Lee and gently pushed Lee's heels outward with his foot, correcting Lee's position.

"Arigato, Sensei!" Lee shouted, thanking Sensei for the correction.

Michael's sore legs were beginning to quiver. It was hard enough to hold a squat when you weren't tired to begin with. How was he supposed to hold the squat after what he'd just been through? And how long was

Sensei going to walk around before he let them do the next move?

"Tight fist, Rosalie," Sensei reminded his daughter, tapping the front of her fist with the palm of his hand.

"Arigato, Sensei!" Rosalie shouted.

"Squat!" Sensei said to Chuck, who sank even lower in his Naihanchi stance.

More corrections? Michael's legs were shaking from the strain, so much that his whole body was vibrating. Any second now, he felt they were going to collapse beneath him. He was trying his best to hold on, but he could tell he wasn't going to make it. He just needed to rest his legs for just for one second, then he'd come back down and squat again. Michael stood up and quickly shook out his legs.

"Is there a problem, Michael?" Sensei asked quietly, focusing his dark brown eyes on him.

Guiltily, Michael sank back down into Naihanchi. "Arigato, Sensei!" he shouted. His legs immediately started to quiver again.

"Are you tired, Michael?" Sensei asked.

"No, Sensei!" Michael lied.

"Good," Sensei said. "Because you're a brown belt now. Very high-ranking student. Brown belts can't rest or come up because they must set a strong example for lower-ranking students."

"Arigato, Sensei!" shouted Michael and some of the other students. Michael felt totally humiliated. Even Dwight, who must have been suffering as badly as he was, hadn't come up.

"And your legs couldn't have been too tired," Sensei went on. "When your body fails, you fall down. When your mind fails, you stand up."

"Arigato, Sensei!" Michael screamed. So this was what it was like to be a brown belt? Michael had always been good at karate. None of his training had prepared him for this, though. He almost felt like crying. He didn't feel like a high-ranking student at all. He felt like the lowest of the low.

"That's prearranged fighting number four," Sensei said. It was a half hour later. Sensei had just demonstrated the basic moves in the mirror, with Lee following behind. Jamie, who already knew prearranged number four, practiced the moves with them also.

Unlike kata, where you blocked and attacked on your own against an imaginary opponent, prearranged fighting was a short sequence of attacks and blocks between two real people. There were five prearranged sequences altogether. Prearranged number one was the simplest. The attacker used three different punches while the defender blocked three different ways. Then the defender would become the attacker, coming back with the same three punches while the other person defended. Now that Lee had earned his black tips, he was allowed to learn prearranged number four. It was a lot trickier than the first three.

A few yards away, the plain brown belts were practicing prearranged number three on their own. Lee glanced quickly toward Michael, who was working with Dwight Vernon. During Naihanchi Sho, Michael had looked so exhausted and wobbly, Lee had been afraid Michael might actually collapse. Michael seemed a little better now, though he was still shaky on his feet.

What Lee realized and Michael didn't was that Sensei had been extra tough on the new brown belts on purpose. Sensei called it "hammering the nail." When people first got their brown belts, they tended to get cocky, just as Michael and Dwight had in the locker room. This, to Sensei, was like a nail sticking up out of the floor. Sensei had to hammer them down with extra tough workouts to make them humble again.

"You two work prearranged number four on your own," Sensei said now to Lee and Jamie. "Jamie, as the more advanced student, feel free to make corrections."

"Arigato, Sensei!" Jamie said, bowing.

Lee, too, drew himself up to attention and bowed. "Arigato, Sensei!"

As Sensei went to watch the other brown belts, Jamie turned to face Lee. Then she bowed again. *"Onegai-shimasu,"* she said. That meant "please teach me." Though Jamie was really the teacher right now, she said "please teach me" because anyone could learn from anyone in karate. Teachers could learn from students, and more advanced students could learn from less advanced. The important thing was to be humble and to keep an open mind.

"Onegai-shimasu, Sempai," Lee said back. *Sempai* was Japanese for senior student. This was how you addressed anyone who had a higher rank than you. The only exception to this was when you addressed Sensei Davis. He was always called Sensei.

"Let's go over the moves slowly," Jamie said. "You attack."

Lee lunged forward on his left leg into a low stance, and his right fist aimed toward Jamie's solar plexus. Right beneath the rib cage, and above the stomach, the solar plexus was one of the most vulnerable targets on the body because it had a lot of nerve endings. A powerful punch or kick there could completely disable an opponent. It was an important place to protect on yourself, and to try to attack on an opponent.

Jamie responded by lunging sideways, to her left, and doing a chest block with her right arm, deflecting Lee's fist. Lee kicked with his right foot toward Jamie's groin. Jamie tucked her right foot behind her left and blocked downward with her right arm.

"Now comes the turn," Jamie said.

Lee and Jamie turned their backs to each other as they pivoted around to face each other from a different angle. Now Lee was set up for his last move, a leaping step forward with his right foot, and another right punch to the solar plexus. The only problem was, he was so far away he'd have to leap nearly five feet to get anywhere near Jamie.

"How'd that happen?" Lee asked.

"That's the tricky part about this prearranged," Jamie said. "It's all about finding the correct distance from your opponent."

"*Ma-ai.*" Lee supplied the term for what Jamie had described.

"Right," Jamie said. "You have to set up the third move just right. If you're too far away, the punch comes up short. And if you're too close, you can't do the punch right either."

"So what did I do wrong?" Lee wanted to know.

"Let's start again," Jamie said. After Lee kicked at her groin, Jamie stopped to watch what Lee did next. "I see," she said, after he'd pivoted. "You're taking too big a step with your right foot. You're almost lunging. It's more of a medium-sized step."

Lee snapped to attention and bowed deeply. "Arigato, Sempai!" he shouted. Then he smiled into Jamie's freckled face and wide-set green eyes. After he'd earned his black tips last Sunday at the promotion, Jamie had asked Lee if he would be her training partner. A training partner was someone of the same rank who you worked with on your kata and prearranged fighting. By working together and correcting each other, you could both improve.

A week ago, Lee never would have believed he'd be smiling at Jamie, let along spending so much time with her. Jamie had recently moved to Midvale from North Carolina. Before Jamie, Lee had been the highest-ranking kid in the dojo. But Jamie had earned her black tips before he had, at her old dojo, which was part of the same karate system.

Lee had felt incredibly jealous of Jamie. Not only was she more advanced, her techniques were much better than his. Lee had been so upset, he'd almost quit karate! Fortunately, though, Sensei had helped Lee realize that karate wasn't about competing with other people. You just had to work on perfecting your *own* techniques.

In the past week, Lee had also realized that he could learn an awful lot from Jamie. She worked out even more often than he did, several hours every day. That had made Lee realize he could work out harder, too. And by trying to copy Jamie's nearly perfect techniques, Lee's techniques were already looking better.

"Can we take it from the kick again, Sempai?" Lee asked Jamie. "I'd like to try that pivoting step again."

"Arigato," Jamie said.

They set up the second move, where Jamie did a down block against Lee's kick. Then Lee tried to take a smaller step as he turned his back on Jamie and set up for the final punch. This time he was much closer. As he took the leaping step forward on his right foot, his right fist came up against Jamie's solar plexus, right where it belonged. Jamie blocked, grabbing his right arm and countering with a right kick aimed at his rib cage.

Lee smiled again at Jamie. It was great having a training partner who could teach him at the same time. Lee couldn't believe he'd ever resented Jamie or wished she hadn't come to Midvale. If one week of working with her had made this much difference, think how much better he'd be a month or a year from now! Thanks to Jamie, Lee loved karate more than ever. Nothing was going to get in the way of his training ever again.

Chapter Four

"Uhhhhhhhh," Michael groaned. It was an hour later, and he was sitting on the wooden bench in the men's locker room. He was staring dumbly at the gray metal lockers, as he had for the past fifteen minutes. It wasn't that the lockers were so interesting. In fact, Michael was tired of looking at them. The problem was, he couldn't get up. His legs were too sore.

"Ohhh," groaned Dwight. He sat next to Michael, also staring at the lockers. "I may never walk again."

Except for Lee, the other brown-belt boys had already dressed and left the dojo. But Michael and Dwight stayed glued to the bench. When Chuck and Nelson were changing, they'd made jokes about "hammering the nail" and laughed while they'd sneaked looks at Michael and Dwight. Michael had

41

had a feeling they'd been talking about him, but he was too exhausted to be embarrassed.

"Maybe I'll call my Mom and ask her to rent a wheelchair so I can get out of here," Dwight said miserably.

"How are you going to get to the phone?" Michael pointed out. "You'd have to walk."

"Oh yeah."

Michael had lost track of how long Sensei had made them hold that Naihanchi squat. And even when Sensei had given the count for them to do the next move, they'd just moved right into another squat. And then another. By the end of class, it had been all Michael and Dwight could do to hobble into the locker room. And now it looked like they might never leave.

"Well," Dwight said finally, "if I don't get home soon, my mother's going to rent out my room." Planting his strong arms on the bench on either side of him, Dwight lifted himself to his feet. "That wasn't so bad . . ." Dwight started to say, but then he took a step. "Agh!" he groaned, clutching his thighs. "Maybe I'm not ready to be a brown belt yet. Maybe I should have waited another six months to test." Slowly, painfully, he shuffled toward the shower and reached in to turn on the water.

"That's what I was thinking," Michael said as

Dwight slowly removed his gi and stepped into the shower. "I don't even know how I'm going to ride my bicycle home . . ." Michael stopped mid-sentence. In all his pain, he'd forgotten that he hadn't ridden his bicycle to class today. He'd taken the bus because they had to go grocery shopping for his parents' surprise party. Which meant he had to get moving right away, pain or no pain.

Michael and his brothers had a lot to accomplish, and they only had a few hours to get it all done. Their parents were going to a flea market this afternoon, and that usually took them hours. It was the perfect time to buy food and do the cooking. They could hide the food in the basement freezer until next Sunday, the date they'd picked for the surprise party.

Jeremy was also going to take the bus and meet them at the dojo after their brown-belt class. He couldn't carry much with one broken hand, but he could help them shop. And he was probably waiting outside right now, which meant Michael had better start getting dressed.

"You want me to leave the water on?" Dwight asked, sticking his head out of the shower. "The hot water feels great!"

Michael nodded. Now all he had to do was stand. Shifting forward so that his bare feet were touching the floor, Michael gently eased himself up and off the bench. His legs screamed in agony as he put his full weight on them. All Michael wanted to do was go home and take a hot bath, but the shower would have to do for now.

And anyway, this was part of his brown-belt training. Sensei Davis may have given a tough class, but Michael wasn't going to be scared off. He may have felt like a cripple, but he was still a deshi. Deshi got the job done, no matter what. Michael was no exception. Leaning against the wall for support, Michael slowly made his way past Dwight to the shower.

Ten minutes later, Michael ran a comb through his wet hair and tossed his stuff into his backpack with his wet gi. He was still moving slowly, but at least he was moving. Which was more than he could say for Lee. Lee hadn't even come into the locker room yet, and class had been over for half an hour.

Where was he? They didn't have much time. If Lee didn't get dressed soon, they wouldn't have enough time to get all their shopping, cooking, and clean-up done before their parents got home.

"You coming?" Dwight asked, grunting as he bent to pick up his gym bag.

"Yeah," Michael answered. His arms ached as he put on his jacket. He slung his backpack painfully over one shoulder and followed Dwight out the curtained doorway leading to the deck.

After bowing to the shinden, Michael looked around for Lee. There he was, in the back of the dojo. He was practicing *jyu-kumite,* or freestyle sparring, with Jamie. Unlike prearranged fighting, where you knew in advance what your opponent was going to do, kumite was unchoreographed. It was more like a real fight, except you pulled all your punches and kicks. The point was to practice, not to hurt your opponent.

"Hyaaaah!" Lee gave a powerful *kiai* as he threw a left snap kick toward Jamie's ribs. Kiai was more than just a loud shout to startle an opponent. Kiai was focusing your mind, your body, and your spirit into one sharp burst of power.

Jamie deflected Lee's kick with a downward strike of her right arm, then countered with a double punch to Lee's solar plexus. Lee darted to the left in cat stance, his weight resting on his bent back leg. At the same time, he blocked against Jamie's arms with knife hands, his fingers straight and stiff and pressed together.

Michael hated to interrupt. The two of them looked like they were having a great time. Lee's gi was soaking wet, and his black hair was plastered to the back of his neck. Jamie's braid had come undone and the knot on her belt was coming loose. But the wall clock said twelve noon, and Michael could see the back of Jeremy's head through the front window of the dojo.

"See ya next week," Michael said to Dwight. Then he padded across the deck in his socks and stood quietly near Lee and Jamie, waiting for them to notice him. Since they were higher-ranking students, it would be impolite to interrupt them, even if Lee *was* his brother.

"Move in closer on that elbow strike," Jamie was saying to Lee. She moved in low and struck upward with her own elbow. "Like that. Take over his space and come up from underneath."

"Arigato, Sempai!" Lee shouted, bowing quickly, then imitating Jamie's move.

Jamie pretended to be struck in the face. She staggered backward, raising her arms long enough for Lee to follow up with a few more kicks to the solar plexus. It looked like they'd never be finished. It also seemed like neither had even noticed Michael. So much for politeness.

"Uh, Lee," Michael called to his brother.

Lee didn't hear at first. He was too busy blocking

his face as Jamie's fist flew toward his nose.

"Lee!" Michael tried again. "Yame!" Yame was Japanese for stop.

At the word *yame,* Jamie and Lee stepped away from each other and turned toward Michael. They were both panting, and there were droplets of sweat all around them on the wooden floor.

"Sorry," Michael said, "but we have to get going. Jeremy's waiting outside."

"Jeremy?" Lee asked. His eyes narrowed, as if he were trying to place the name. Michael shook his head. Lee had always been a little fanatical about karate, but he'd gotten even worse since he got his black tips. Sometimes it seemed like Lee's head was so filled with karate, there wasn't room for anything else.

"Our brother, remember?" Michael said pointedly.

Lee's eyes focused and he nodded. "Sorry."

"So get dressed," Michael said. "Remember our secret mission this afternoon?"

"Oh yeah, the party," Lee said slowly. "I guess we'd better go." He didn't move, though, and cast a sideways look at Jamie. Michael knew what Lee was thinking. Lee wanted to work out just a little longer. Michael knew the feeling. He got it every time he was in the middle of drawing one of his comic book characters and his mother interrupted to make him take out the garbage or something. Michael hated to be interrupted.

"Tell you what," Michael said. "Jeremy and I will meet you at the grocery store. But don't be too long, okay?"

"You're the best," Lee said, giving Michael a light punch on the shoulder. "I'll be out of here in five minutes."

Lee and Jamie bowed to each other and took passive fighting stance to begin sparring again. Michael, meanwhile, painfully made his way toward the door, bowed again to the shinden, and stepped into the hall. Grabbing his sneakers, Michael just jammed his feet inside without trying them. Then he pushed open the front door and saw Jeremy waiting . . . with his bicycle.

"Jeremy!" Michael exclaimed, approaching his brother. "What did you bring your bike for? You were supposed to take the bus so you could help us take the groceries home. That was part of the plan. We can't take your bike on the bus!"

Jeremy nervously pushed his glasses up on his nose. "Sorry," he said. "I forgot."

"And what about your cast?" Michael added, pointing to Jeremy's right arm. "You know Mom and Dad said not to ride with it. What if you fall?"

"You sound just like Mom and Dad," Jeremy grumbled.

"You should be happy I'm not," Michael said. "If they knew, you'd get in big trouble."

Jeremy's freckled face turned bright red. "You better not tell," he said heatedly. "I ride great with one hand."

Michael sighed. "Come on," he said, grabbing the handlebars of Jeremy's bike. He wheeled it down the concrete walk toward Mega-Mart, trying to ignore the pain in his legs. Jeremy fell into step beside him. "Of course I won't tell," Michael told his younger brother.

"Where's Lee?" Jeremy asked as they passed Plaza Shoes, Landmark Dry Cleaners, and World o' Donuts.

"Sparring with Jamie," Michael said. "But he's going to meet us in a few minutes."

"I read the master party plan you left me this morning," Jeremy said. "Pretty impressive."

"Thanks," Michael said. "So, what do you think we should make? I was thinking nachos for appetizers, then enchiladas and burritos for dinner, and chocolate cake with chocolate icing for dessert. I can do the main course today while Mom and Dad are at the flea market, then Wednesday when they go out we can bake the cake. We can make the nachos Sunday, the morning of the party, after Grandma gets them out of the house."

"Whoa, whoa," Jeremy said, holding up his cast arm. "That's way too much work. We might not even get the enchiladas done before Mom and Dad get home. I checked out the recipe. It takes hours, and you have to melt the cheese and make this special sauce."

"Well, do you have a better idea?" Michael snapped. He didn't mean to sound so grumpy, but every step he took was agony. And now Jeremy was trying to wreck his perfect plan.

With his good hand, Jeremy reached into the pocket of his jeans and rummaged around. He removed an eraser in the shape of a football, some paper clips, a dime, three pennies, and a piece of fluff before he came up with a dirty, folded piece of paper. "Here it is," he said, handing it to Michael. "Look." Jeremy took hold of the handlebars with his left hand while Michael unfolded the paper.

Michael read Jeremy's shaky handwriting:

Grandma Kussack's Famous Chili

2 pounds chipped hamburger meat
2 cans tomato prse
Some onions
Spices (call Grandma)
Peepers

(Feeds eight)

"Excuse me?" Michael asked, looking at Jeremy. "What's this supposed to be?"

"It's Grandma's famous chili," Jeremy explained. "I called her this morning for the recipe. Mom and Dad like Mexican food, and this is a lot easier than making enchiladas."

"That's true," Michael admitted.

"Grandma even said she'd make it," Jeremy added. "You know how much she loves to cook."

"I know, I know," Michael said. "But this is *our* party for *our* parents, so we should be the ones doing this."

Jeremy shrugged. "Just trying to save time and trouble."

51

"It's no trouble," Michael said. "But maybe you're right. Chili would be easier to make. We'll have to make, like, three times as much, though."

By now, the boys had reached Mega-Mart, probably the world's largest supermarket. Nearly the size of a football field, it sold groceries, books, toys, appliances, and even lawn furniture. Weaving through rows of jammed-together shopping carts, Michael found the bike rack and locked Jeremy's bike. Then they entered through one of the dozen automatic, sliding glass doors.

"How's Lee going to find us?" Jeremy asked as they headed inside the gleaming white store. There were at least twenty cashiers whisking items across red laser scanners as they rang up purchases. Behind the cashiers were seemingly endless rows of neon-colored boxes, bottles, and cans stacked nearly to the ceiling.

"He'll find us," Michael assured Jeremy. "Meanwhile, let's start getting what we need from the list." He checked the recipe again. "What's chipped hamburger?"

"Sorry," Jeremy said, grabbing an empty grocery cart. "It is supposed to be chopped. I'm still not writing too well with my left hand." Michael was amazed that Jeremy could write at all. Jeremy was right-handed, but he'd adapted pretty quickly to writing with his other hand.

"No problem," Michael said, looking up at the bright red signs that hung above each aisle. "Where's the meat section?"

After they'd put a little over six pounds of hamburger packages in their cart, Michael and Jeremy found an aisle with nothing but cans of tomato products. There was tomato paste, tomato sauce, tomato puree, whole tomatoes in their own juice, chopped tomatoes, and cans with writing in Italian that Michael couldn't understand. Michael checked the recipe again.

"Tomato prse?" he asked. "What's that?"

Jeremy took the paper from Michael and studied it. "You know," he said, "I don't remember. It's something with a *p*. Paste? Puree? I dunno."

Michael felt himself growing more anxious by the second as Jeremy wondered aloud. Still, he tried to remain calm. "Think," he prompted Jeremy. "What did Grandma say?"

Jeremy screwed up his mouth and frowned. "Sorry," he said. "I'm really not into this cooking stuff." Then his face brightened. "I know," he said. "Why don't we get both? Then we're covered either way."

Michael took the master party plan out of his knapsack and turned to the first page of numbers, where he'd figured out the budget. They had almost sixty dollars, but the meat alone cost about fifteen. Still, they could probably afford it.

"Okay," Michael said. "We'll get both." He pushed the cart down the aisle until he found bright red cans of tomato puree. There was just one problem. The cans came in all different sizes, from little six ouncers up to the gigantic economy size.

"Uh oh," Jeremy said, realizing the problem.

"Did Grandma say what size can?" Michael asked Jeremy, already knowing the answer. Grandma Kussack didn't like to be bothered with details. She was too busy, she always said. And Michael was sure Jeremy hadn't thought to ask.

"Like I said," Jeremy started to apologize, "I'm not really into this cooking stuff."

"I know, I know," Michael said. "Okay. We'll just have to guess, I guess." Michael grabbed the biggest size of tomato puree and hefted it into the shopping cart. The thing must have weighed at least a couple of pounds. "This ought to be enough," Michael said. Then he nudged the cart a few feet forward toward the tomato paste.

"So where's Lee?" Jeremy asked as they left the

tomato section and headed toward the fruit and vegetable department. Pyramids of green apples and yellow grapefruit and bright red tomatoes were stacked dangerously high on either side.

Michael glanced around. He saw a mother pushing a shopping cart and trying to keep track of five small children at the same time. He saw a confused-looking old lady wandering around with a box of Q-tips. But there was no sign of Lee. Michael checked his watch. He'd left the dojo fifteen minutes ago. Lee should have had plenty of time to get here by now.

"He's probably lost in this place," Michael said. "I'm sure he'll show up any second."

When they reached the onions, Michael checked Grandma's recipe again. "*Some* onions?" he asked, looking down his nose at Jeremy.

Jeremy grimaced. "Sorry," he said. "I guess I was supposed to ask how many, right?"

Half an hour later, Michael and Jeremy loaded their groceries onto the black rubber conveyor belt at the cashier's station. Michael had allowed Jeremy to talk him into substituting potato chips and popcorn for cooked appetizers, and he'd bought a prepared mix and canned icing for the cake. Michael felt bad about not making everything from scratch, but they didn't have enough money to do it any other way.

"That'll be fifty-eight sixty-three," said the cashier, holding out her hand for Michael's money.

Michael gave her fifty-eight dollars, all the paper money he had, then dug around in his pocket for change. He could only come up with fifty cents.

"Here," Jeremy said, digging up his dime and three pennies again and adding them to Michael's change.

"Thanks," Michael said as he and Jeremy pushed through the narrow aisle between cashier stations. The man bagging the groceries placed the last of their bags on the end of the counter. There were six altogether, and they looked heavy.

"Need a cart to get these out of here?" the man asked.

"Uh-uh," Jeremy assured him. "We can carry them. After all, we're deshi, right?" he added to Michael.

"Mmm-hmmm," Michael answered absently as he scanned the front of the store for Lee. He didn't see him anywhere.

"So where's Lee?" Jeremy asked again, echoing Michael's thought.

Michael peered through the glass doors to see if Lee was waiting for them outside, but he wasn't there either. What could have happened to him? Lee had always been dependable, and he hadn't had to go far to get here from the dojo.

"Excuse me," said a voice behind Michael, "but I'm trying to get out."

Michael turned and saw the mother with the five children behind him. She was carrying a bag of groceries, and she looked impatient.

"Oh, sorry," Michael said, stepping aside so she could pass. They couldn't stand here and block the aisle all day. But as Michael looked from his own two hands, to Jeremy's one good one, to the six heavy bags of groceries, he realized they had a serious problem. It wouldn't be so bad getting the bags out of the grocery store. That they could manage with a little planning. But how were they ever going to get all this stuff home without Lee?

Chapter Five

"I can carry two bags with one hand," Jeremy volunteered, flexing his left arm to show off his biceps. "Maybe even three."

Michael rolled his eyes. It was a nice offer, but there was no way Jeremy could make good on it. Two of the bags had the enormous cans of tomato stuff, and the others were filled with heavy containers of juice and soda. Jeremy would be lucky if he could carry one bag.

"We'll have to make a couple trips to get these out of the store," Michael said. "But that's as far as we're going to get without Lee. *Where is he?*"

Jeremy stooped down and grabbed one of the heavier bags. "I know," he said as Michael picked up another bag in each hand. "We'll walk these outside, then I'll watch the bags while you take my bike back to the dojo to look for him."

Michael nodded. "That's the only way this is going to work, I guess," he sighed. Dodging other shoppers and a line of people waiting to return deposit bottles, the brothers made their way out of the store. "I'll get the rest," Michael told Jeremy as they plunked bags down on the sidewalk.

Michael's arms were aching almost as badly as his legs by the time he'd carried the rest of the bags outside. Then he unlocked Jeremy's bicycle. "I'll probably pass Lee on the way here," he said, hopping on. "Keep an eye on the bags."

"No sweat," Jeremy said. He leaned over and pulled a package of Oreos out of a grocery bag and started to open it with his teeth.

"Hey!" Michael said. "Those are for the party!"

"Sorry," Jeremy said. "I just wanted to keep busy while I was waiting. I should have brought something to read."

"I'll be right back!" Michael exclaimed. "Read the signs in the windows if you get bored."

Michael pushed off and rode away on Jeremy's bike. His legs were still burning so much from class that it was hard to press against the pedals. As he carefully steered around the parking lot, he tried to ignore the pain and keep his eyes peeled for Lee. Any second, Michael expected to see his brother running toward him, hair flying in the wind, as he rushed to the grocery store. But there was no sign of him.

When he got to the dojo, Michael locked the bicycle and pulled open the door. The front hallway was empty, but Michael recognized Lee's basketball sneakers sitting on an empty shelf in the shoe closet. Jamie's scuffed brown cowboy boots were there, too, on the floor. What was going on?

Michael stuck his head through the curtained doorway leading to the deck. What he saw in the back of the room made his heart start to pound and his chest feel tight.

"Point your toe more," Jamie was saying to Lee as she demonstrated a front snap kick. "Think of *piercing* your opponent, not just pushing him back with your foot." Lee stood nearby, watching, looking happy and exhausted.

Lee and Jamie were still sparring! Michael couldn't believe it! Forty-five minutes ago, Lee had said he'd be off the deck right away. Lee had promised to help them. But here he was, exactly as Michael had left him.

"Lee!" Michael shouted. "What are you still doing here?"

Lee pulled his eyes away from Jamie's kick. As soon as Lee saw Michael, his happy look disappeared. "Uh oh," he said, bowing quickly to Jamie and running toward Michael. "What time is it?"

Michael nodded toward the wall clock. It was nearly one o'clock already.

Lee bit his lower lip. "I'm really sorry!" he said, untying the knot of his brown belt. "I guess I lost track of the time. I'll be right out to help you shop." He took off across the deck toward the men's locker room.

"Too late," Michael called, following Lee. "It's already done. But we can't carry all the bags without you."

Lee stopped abruptly and bowed toward Jamie, who still stood in the back of the room. "Arigato, Sempai!" he said. "Gotta go."

"Arigato," she said, bowing and giving a little wave. "See you Monday."

Lee picked up the pace again and burst into the empty locker room. "I can't believe I did this!" he exclaimed, throwing his belt on the wooden bench and peeling off his gi. "It's like I was on another planet

61

or something. I hope you're not too mad at me. I
promise this will never happen again." He stepped
into the shower, and Michael heard the water go on.
"I'll be right out!" he promised.

Michael's lips were pressed together, and he was
breathing through his nose. For a split second, he
crazily thought about flushing the toilet next to the
shower so the water raining down on Lee would get
scalding hot. But that was dumb.

Lee hadn't let them down on purpose. He just got
caught up in something that meant a lot to him.
Michael and Jeremy loved karate, but karate was
practically Lee's *life*. And Michael wasn't the only
one who'd just earned a new rank and was trying to
prove himself. Lee had just gotten his black tips,
which was an even bigger deal than getting a brown
belt. Lee had the whole school looking up to him as
an example. No wonder Lee wanted to spend all his
time with Jamie, working on his technique.

"Done!" Lee announced, stepping out of the
shower, quickly drying himslf off with his towel, and
throwing on his clothes. He crushed his wet gi into
his backpack without bothering to fold it neatly, as
he usually did. "What do you want me to do?" Lee
asked, grabbing up his backpack and combing his hair
with his fingers at the same time. "I'm all yours."

Lee did seem genuinely sorry. There was no point rubbing it in. "Jeremy's waiting with the groceries," Michael said, heading for the doorway leading to the deck. "But he brought his bike so one of us will have to ride it home for him. Two of us can take the groceries on the bus."

"Gotcha," Lee said as he hurried across the deck. Michael tried to keep up, but his legs had run out of energy for today. "I guess I should be the one to ride the bike." He gave Michael a sly glance.

"What's that supposed to mean?" Michael asked as they pushed through the curtain into the front hallway.

Lee smiled a little as he grabbed his sneakers and dropped them on the floor. "Oh, nothing," he said. "I just thought your legs might be a little sore today, that's all."

Michael didn't like the look on Lee's face. Come to think of it, it looked a lot like the ones Nelson and Chuck were giving him earlier, in the locker room. Was there something going on here that Michael didn't know about? Did they all think Michael was some sort of weakling since he'd stood up for a few seconds in class?

"My legs are fine," Michael insisted. "*I'll* take the bike. I rode it here, you know. You just take care of

Jeremy and the groceries. We'd better hurry, too. Mom and Dad should be home by four o'clock. I've got to get the chili cooked by then."

After they'd left the dojo, Michael unlocked Jeremy's bike. Though the last thing he wanted was to use his legs to pedal again, he straddled the bike and rode, ahead of Lee, toward Mega-Mart. Now it was Lee's turn to try to keep up.

"I hope Jeremy hasn't eaten all the Oreos," Michael said, scanning the walkway as he coasted toward Mega-Mart.

"Tell me about it," Lee said, jogging to keep pace with the bike. "I know he's got his cast on and he's not supposed to ride, but leaving Jeremy with six bags of groceries might have been a big mistake." Besides science fiction and karate, eating was Jeremy's favorite pastime.

"He'd better not have eaten it all," Michael said, " 'cause we're out of money. We can't afford to buy any more."

Michael squeezed the brakes as they neared Mega-Mart. They were coming up on the place where he'd left Jeremy, but so far Michael couldn't see him. There were a lot of people walking around, though. Jeremy was probably lost in the crowd.

Hopping off the bike, Michael looked around for

his brother. "Jeremy!" he called, but he got no response. "I don't get it," Michael said to Lee. "I left him right—"

Michael's left foot banged into something. He looked down. He'd just made a dent in the side of a grocery bag. Next to it was another one, then four more, lined up neatly against the front of a store. Michael was starting to get a funny feeling in his stomach.

"What's the matter?" Lee asked.

Michael glanced into the bags. Yup. There was the tomato paste. *And* the tomato puree. Potato chips and popcorn, too. But there was no Jeremy. "These are ours," Michael explained to Lee, starting to breathe fast through his nose again.

"Then where's Jeremy?" Lee asked. "Why would he leave—"

"Hi, you guys!" Jeremy called to them as he pushed open the door of the store right next to Mega-Mart. He was carrying a yellow plastic bag.

Michael stared at Jeremy in disbelief. " 'Hi, you guys?' That's all you have to say? What about the fact that you left sixty dollars' worth of groceries just sitting on the sidewalk for anyone to steal? What about the fact that you said you were going to watch them and you didn't?"

"I had my eye on them all the time," Jeremy insisted. "Beverly's has a glass window."

Now Michael looked more closely at Jeremy's bag. It was made of yellow plastic and had the logo *Beverly's Book Corner*. There was an outline of something rectangular inside it. "What's that?" Michael asked.

Jeremy grinned and pulled out a large paperback book. On the cover was an illustration of a silver spaceship and six cartoon humans, androids, and aliens in green and gold uniforms. The title said, in bright red letters, *Galaxy Voyagers: The First Five Years*. "I'm glad you told me to read the signs in the windows!" he exclaimed. Jeremy flipped through the book with his left hand while he balanced it against his right arm. "It's got every single comic strip from the day *Galaxy Voyagers* first started."

"I thought you cut out all the *Galaxy Voyagers* comic strips from the newspaper," Lee said. "You have them already in a scrapbook."

"But these are in color," Jeremy explained.

Michael suddenly thought of something. "Let me see that," he said to Jeremy. Jeremy handed him the book and Michael turned it until he found the cover price. Eleven dollars and ninety-five cents. Where had Jeremy come up with that kind of money? In the grocery store, they hadn't been able to buy everything they wanted because they'd run out of money. And just yesterday, Jeremy had said he could only contribute eight dollars and eighty-seven cents to the party because that was all he had.

"Did you hold out on us?" Michael asked Jeremy. "We were supposed to use all our money for the party."

Jeremy grabbed the book back and shoved it in the bag. "This doesn't count! I've been saving up for this for months."

Michael felt a raw nerve twitching on the side of his head, as if someone was tapping a straight pin into his skull. The nerve sent jagged pulses of pain through his entire body. Michael's chest heaved up and down as he felt himself breathe faster.

Michael took a deep breath and tried to relax. "It's okay," he told Jeremy. "Nothing was stolen. And I guess you wanted the book a long time before we planned the party."

Jeremy breathed a sigh of relief. "So you're not mad?"

Michael noticed a city bus pulling into the parking lot at the other end of the mall. It would take a few minutes for the bus to get down to this end, but they still had work to do. "Let's just get all these bags to

67

the bus stop," Michael said. He bent down and grabbed two of the bags in one arm and one bag in the other. Lee grabbed two more, and Jeremy grabbed the last one.

"I'll help load you on," Michael said as the bus made its first stop at the other end of the mall. "Then I'll ride Jeremy's bike to the bus stop near our house and help you carry them the rest of the way home."

"Sorry about the bike," Jeremy said again as they struggled with their loads to the green wooden bench at the bus stop.

As the bus approached, Michael's heart jumped. "Oh no! I just remembered," he gasped. "We don't have any money left. How are you guys gonna pay?"

Lee put his bags down and fished around in the side pocket of his backpack. "I have some change," he said calmly. He pulled out some dimes and quarters and quickly added them up. "Lucky break," he said. "Just enough for two."

The bus pulled up and exhaled with a *whoosh* as the door opened. Jeremy got on first, followed by Lee who put the money in for both of them. Jeremy carried one bag while Lee juggled two. As Michael climbed the stairs after them, he saw that there were so many people on the bus all the seats were taken and people were even jamming the aisle in the middle.

How were they going to put all the grocery bags down?

"Hey!" the driver said to Michael. "You didn't pay."

"I'm not taking the bus," Michael started to explain. "I'm just trying to—"

"Then don't block the door," the driver said. "Other people are trying to get on."

Michael looked for Lee and Jeremy, but they'd squeezed through the people in front of the bus and had disappeared. "Lee!" Michael called. "What about the bags?"

"Leave 'em!" Lee called from the back. "I'll pick 'em up on my way out."

"No you don't," the driver said as Michael tried to find room to put them on the floor. "Pal, there's not enough room for the passengers. Fugettabout some bags. You'll have to take them with you."

"But . . ." Michael started to plead.

"Read my lips, kid," the bus driver said right over him. "You and the bags: off!"

Michael backed down the steps and let the grocery bags thud to the pavement. As the bus pulled away, the nerve in his head started to pulse more sharply. Michael felt like his skull would split apart.

This is all part of my training, Michael thought as

he picked up the bags again and walked them over to Jeremy's bicycle. He was a deshi. He would screen out everything else. He'd only focus on figuring out how to get all these groceries home.

Jeremy had a wire basket attached to the front of his handlebars and leather saddlebags hanging over the sides of the back wheel. The basket was small, though. Michael was only able to wedge in a few bags of potato chips and some happy anniversary napkins. The saddlebags were even smaller. Michael got paper plates into one and the onions into the other. That still left two bags' worth.

I can do it, Michael urged himself on. *This should be nothing compared to all those deep knee bends and squatting.* He slung one bag over the right handlebar and the other bag over the left. Then he got on the bike and tried to pedal, but it was impossible to balance with all the extra weight and the bags banging against his knees.

As Michael walked the bicycle and the groceries home, he tried to control his breathing, the way they did in class, to calm himself and clear his mind. *In through the nose, out through the mouth,* Sensei Davis always said. *Inhale strength, exhale weakness.*

It was starting to work, too. Michael was already seeing things more clearly. He couldn't expect Lee and Jeremy to take as much responsibility as he did. After all, they were younger than he was. *He* was the oldest. It was *his* job to make sure the party was a success.

As Michael started up the steep hill behind the mall's parking lot, he smiled. He was already feeling much better. But it was still a long way home.

Chapter Six

"I never want to look at food again as long as I live," Jeremy groaned as he let his grocery bag thump to the blue and white linoleum floor. "My arm is killing me!" He raised his left arm above his head and circled it forward and then back, like they did in karate class to loosen up.

Your arm? Michael wanted to say. *What about mine?* Jeremy had only carried one bag, and he'd had it on the bus most of the time. Michael's own arms had been nearly wrenched out of their sockets from the weight of the two bags he'd carried from the bus stop, plus he'd had to push the bike. His arms were stiff, too, because the bags had cut off his circulation.

Michael wasn't about to give in to weakness or pain, though. There wasn't time. It was a quarter to two.

They had about two hours to make the chili. *And* clean up afterward. It was going to be mighty tight.

"I'll get out the big pot Dad uses for spaghetti sauce," Michael said, putting down his bags. "Lee, you start chopping the onions, and Jeremy, you read the recipe out loud."

"Can we get something to eat first?" Jeremy asked, yanking open the refrigerator. "I'm starving!"

"I thought you never wanted to see food again," Lee teased.

"Ha ha ha," Jeremy said, pulling out a carton of orange juice. Then he reached into the cookie jar and pulled out some chocolate chip cookies. Juggling all of this, he walked over to the table, sat down, and put up his feet.

"You comfortable?" Michael asked with a glare.

Jeremy started to nod, then he remembered the recipe. "Oh! Sorry," he said, pulling the grimy paper from his pocket. "Okay, here goes. For Grandma Kussack's Famous Chili, take two pounds chopped hamburger meat—"

"Skip the ingredients," Michael said, pulling the deep covered pot out of a low cabinet and putting it on top of the stove. "Just read the directions."

"Okay." Jeremy popped two cookies in his mouth

at once—whole. He started to read as he chewed. "Sote the onions in oil. . . . Sote? What does that mean?"

Michael walked over to Jeremy and looked at the paper. "Sauté," he corrected Jeremy. "It's pronounced saw-TAY. That means fry."

"Oh." Jeremy continued, "Then add the peppers and hamburger meat. Stir until brown. Then add tomato stuff, puree or paste, I'm not sure which one, add spices, and let simmer for an hour or two."

"An hour or two!" Michael shouted. "We better hurry. You got those onions ready, Lee?"

Lee had set up the wooden chopping board on the kitchen counter. Now he was peeling the onions and sniffling. "My eyes are killing me!" he complained, wiping away tears. "I can't even see straight."

"It's the onions," Michael said. "Speaking of which, we still don't know how many we need. And what kind of oil do we fry them in?"

Jeremy shrugged. "It doesn't say. I guess we should call Grandma."

"Good idea." Michael picked up the phone and punched out the numbers. He got a busy signal. "She's on the phone," Michael said. "Now what do we do?"

"Maybe we should wait," Jeremy suggested. "I'm really tired from everything we've done already. Why don't we just hide the food and cook it another day when Mom and Dad aren't home?"

"I'm with Jeremy," Lee said, yawning wide. "We still have a week until the party. We don't have to do everything today. And to tell you the truth, I'm kind of beat from all that sparring with Jamie. I might even take a nap."

Michael looked from Lee, yawning and sniffling, to Jeremy, chewing with his mouth open and dropping crumbs on the floor. It was hard to believe they were deshi. Didn't they realize that karate training didn't stop when you left the dojo? You were supposed to be a warrior all the time. That meant you couldn't give in to pain. You had to be strong no matter what the obstacles were. Lee may have had a higher rank than Michael, but it was clearly up to Michael to set a good example here.

"I don't care what you guys do," he said, "but I'm going to cook this chili before Mom and Dad get home. I need the rest of the day anyway to work on my family portrait. If you guys don't want to help me, fine." He opened the pantry cabinet and started looking through the bottles of oil. There was corn oil, peanut oil, and safflower oil. Michael pulled out all the bottles and lined them up on the counter.

Looking guilty, Lee opened a drawer and pulled

out the chopping knife. "Well, I guess I could at least finish chopping the onions."

"And I'll try Grandma again," Jeremy said, getting up off his chair. While Jeremy made the call, Michael got the rest of the chili ingredients out of the grocery bags. "It's ringing," Jeremy said, handing the receiver to Michael.

"Hello?" Grandma Kussack's voice came over the line.

"Hi, Grandma, it's Michael."

"So?" Grandma asked. "How's the chili?"

"That's why I'm calling," Michael said. "Some of the directions were kind of vague. I was wondering if you could clear up a couple points for me." Michael lifted the extension cord over Jeremy's head as he crossed the kitchen to find a pencil. Michael wanted to be able to take down Grandma's directions so he wouldn't forget.

"Why don't you just let me make it for you?" Grandma asked reasonably. "It would take me five minutes! You know me—I love to cook. I'll bring it next Sunday."

Michael found a pencil in a drawer next to the refrigerator. He grabbed the directions out of Jeremy's hand and went over to a counter. "We already bought the stuff," Michael said. "Besides, we *want* to do this. It's for Mom and Dad."

"You're getting to be such a big boy!" Grandma exclaimed, managing to make Michael feel like exactly the opposite. "But you've always been responsible. Remember the time both your parents had the flu and couldn't get out of bed? You made breakfast for your brothers every morning for a week and got them off to school. How old were you then? Seven? Eight?"

"Nine," Michael said shortly. "So, those directions?"

"What do you want to know?"

"Well, what kind of oil do we fry in?"

"Oh, it doesn't matter," Grandma said. "I just use whatever I have around."

Jeremy pulled on the phone cord and waved his hand in front of Michael's face. "Psssst!" he said. "I'm going to hide the munchies and soda in the basement so Mom and Dad don't see them."

Michael gave Jeremy the thumbs up. "Is corn oil okay?" he asked, getting back to his conversation with Grandma.

"Sure," she said. "What else?"

"Well, do I use tomato paste, or tomato puree?"

"They're both good," Grandma said. "Sometimes I use both."

Michael was beginning to wonder if calling Grandma would really clear things up. "Okay," he said. "But how much do I use?"

"It depends on how much you're making. To serve eight, I usually use a can."

"What size?"

"Oh, the little one, you know. About so big."

Michael had the feeling Grandma was demonstrating with her hands, but unfortunately he couldn't see them. "I'm tripling your recipe," he said. "How much do you think that would be?"

"About three cups of tomato puree," Grandma said, finally giving Michael something he could write down. "Then add about three cups of water. If it gets too thick, add some more water."

"Great," Michael said. "Thanks a lot."

"You want me to come over there and help you?" Grandma asked. "I could be there in five minutes."

Actually, Grandma lived about ten minutes away, but she had a tendency to drive a little too fast. "We'll be fine," Michael said.

"Well, call me if you have any more questions."

After Michael hung up, he noticed that Lee had

finished chopping the onions *and* the peppers. "Thanks," he told his brother, who was now yawning with every other breath.

"Do you mind if I go upstairs and lie down for a little while?" Lee asked. "There's not much left to do, is there?"

Michael checked the recipe again. With all the vegetables chopped, it seemed like the only thing left was to sauté everything in stages and add tomato puree. "I guess I can take it from here," Michael said.

"I feel bad leaving you with all the work," Lee said. "I'll just lie down for a few minutes, then I'll come back and help you."

"Sure," Michael said. "Thanks."

After Lee had wandered sluggishly out of the kitchen, Michael wondered where Jeremy had gone. Was he still in the basement? Or had he gone upstairs? Well, it didn't really matter. Michael would be fine on his own. Michael checked his watch. Five after two. Time to kick into high gear.

Michael poured some corn oil into the deep pot on the stove and turned on the gas flame. When the oil started to heat up, he tossed in the peppers and onions. A mouth-watering smell reached up toward his nostrils as he stirred the vegetables with a wooden spoon. Michael checked his watch again. Ten after two. He had to hurry and brown the meat so it would have two hours to sit in the sauce and spices.

Spices! Michael checked the recipe again. All it said was to call Grandma. And Michael hadn't bought any spices in the grocery store. He could only hope he had what he needed right here.

Two hours and several phone calls to Grandma later, Michael had a bubbly pot of chili that filled the kitchen with a steamy, spicy aroma. He'd almost scorched the meat and slightly overcooked the onions, and his brothers never came back, but none of it mattered. The important thing was that Michael had done the job. Now all he had to do was transfer the chili to a big Tupperware container he'd set out on the counter, and he'd be home free.

Beep! Beep!

Michael froze. That was the horn on his dad's Jeep. His parents were home! And the chili was still sitting on the stove! Not to mention the dirty pot and utensils in the sink. Then Michael heard the rumble of the electric garage door opening. Any minute now, his parents would be walking through the door. Michael had to get rid of the evidence fast, but there was no time. Oh no! It looked like after all his hard and frantic work, Michael was going to be caught red-handed!

Chapter Seven

No! Michael told himself. He couldn't let his parents spoil the surprise. Not after everything he'd been through.

With a superhuman burst of speed, Michael went into action. Grabbing the heavy pot, he turned it upside down and emptied the chili into the oversize Tupperware container. He accidentally slopped a little chili over the sides and onto the counter, but he didn't have time to worry about that just yet. Michael pushed down the plastic Tupperware lid and threw open the cabinet beneath the sink. The cabinet was filled with Windex and Ajax and silver polish, but if he pushed back some of the cans and bottles, there was just enough room for the chili.

Michael heard the Jeep as it pulled into the garage. He had only seconds left, and there were still dirty pots in the sink and chili mess all over the stove and counters. Not to mention the cutting board, knife, onion peels, and empty cans of tomato puree. He had to get rid of all of it—fast. Too bad he couldn't throw it away.

That was it! Michael opened a drawer and yanked out a large garbage bag. Moving like he was on fast forward, Michael raced through the kitchen, dumping everything he'd used into the bag. Then he twisted the top of the bag and tied it in a knot.

The Jeep engine shut off. Now all his parents had to do was get out of the car and walk a few feet to the door that separated the garage from the kitchen.

Clanking and clattering, Michael dragged the garbage bag full of pots toward the door leading down to the basement. With a tremendous heave, he threw the bag down the stairs and shut the door quickly behind him to muffle the horrible crash as the bag landed at the bottom.

Michael heard two car doors slam, then approaching footsteps.

Grabbing a wet sponge, Michael frantically wiped up the countertop and the stove, turning the yellow sponge a reddish orange with chili juice. Even Turbotron, the comic book superhero, couldn't have moved any faster.

By the time the door from the garage started to open, the kitchen was gleaming white again, and spotless. Now all Michael had to do was slow his heart down so he could speak without gasping for breath.

"You got it?" Mr. Jenkins asked as Mrs. Jenkins backed up the step into the kitchen. Andrea Jenkins was wearing a pink sweatshirt, jeans, and sneakers, and she seemed to be carrying something heavy. She wasn't very tall, but she was strong from regular workouts at the gym. Her coppery red hair was pulled back into a ponytail.

"No problem," she said, backing farther into the kitchen.

Stephen Jenkins, Michael's father, followed carrying the other end of what Michael could now see was a table. Mr. Jenkins was tall and muscular, with sandy straight hair like Michael's and round, wire-rimmed glasses like Jeremy's. A retired army officer, he ran the local recycling center.

Still breathing hard, Michael saw that the table had a marble top and fancy carved gold legs. It was exactly the sort of table Michael's mother loved and his father hated because it was too frilly and fluffy looking. Michael's dad called stuff like this "wicky wocky," and Michael tended to agree. But he was grateful his parents were paying attention to something else besides the kitchen.

"Mmmmmm!" Mrs. Jenkins said as she and Mr. Jenkins lowered the table to the linoleum floor. She turned around to face Michael. "What's that delicious smell? Chili?"

The smell! Michael had been so busy cleaning up he'd forgotten all about the spicy, meaty odor that filled the kitchen. It was a total giveaway. Just like the wooden spoon still sitting on the far end of the counter, limp, damp onion bits still clinging to it. Michael's heart sank down into his feet. In his rush, he'd missed the spoon, too. But he still wasn't willing to give up.

"Uh, no," Michael said, charging across the kitchen to block his parents' view of the spoon. "It's uh . . ." Michael searched for a believable excuse. What smelled like chili but wasn't chili? "Sloppy Joe!" he shouted. "I made a Sloppy Joe for lunch. Sorry I didn't save you any."

It was time to change the subject. "Nice table!" Michael lied. "You pick that up at the flea market?"

Mr. Jenkins rolled his eyes. "It wasn't my idea. Look at the little flowers carved into the legs and all

84

the curlicues. It's too wicky wocky, and we certainly don't need another table."

"You don't know what you're talking about," Mrs. Jenkins insisted. "It's gorgeous. You just don't appreciate fine workmanship."

"But where are we going to put it?" Mr. Jenkins said, looking at the table as if he'd like to put it in front of the house for the garbage pickup.

Mrs. Jenkins placed her hands protectively on the marble top which, Michael now noticed, was a very feminine shade of pink. Just perfect for a house full of men. "It will go perfectly in the upstairs hallway, against the empty wall. That wall *needs* something, don't you think?"

This was the chance Michael had been waiting for. Though this table was the last thing he wanted to see every morning as he stumbled across the hall to the bathroom, his mother had said the magic word. *Upstairs*. If agreeing with his mother would get his parents out of the kitchen, Michael was prepared to say anything.

"I think it would look *great!*" Michael said enthusiastically, patting the table with affection. "In fact, I can't wait to see how great it looks up there. Let's take it up there *right now!*" Michael grabbed the edge of the pink marble top and tried to pull the table single-handedly across the kitchen floor, but the thing must have weighed a hundred pounds. He could barely move it two inches.

"Hey, hey!" his dad said. "It's too heavy. You'll hurt yourself."

"At least *someone* in this family has some taste," Mrs. Jenkins said with a sniff.

"Okay," Mr. Jenkins grumbled. "We'll take it upstairs. I don't know how I let you talk me into this."

Michael's parents stooped down to pick up the table again. Wanting to make it as easy as possible for them to leave the room, Michael pushed the kitchen door wide open and directed them toward the front hall like a traffic cop.

"Because you're a wonderful person who wants his wife to have a special anniversary present," Mrs. Jenkins said sweetly as the two of them slowly made their way toward the stairs. "Besides, it was a bargain!"

Strong as both his parents were, it seemed to take forever for them to get the table up the stairs. And Michael didn't dare go back to the kitchen until he was sure they were out of sight and out of hearing range. At last, Michael saw his father's workboots disappear around the corner at the top of the stairs. This was Michael's cue.

Racing back into the kitchen, he grabbed the wooden spoon off the counter and skidded to a halt in front of the sink. Throwing open the cabinet, he grabbed the giant container of chili and bolted for the door leading down to the cellar. Michael practically fell down the stairs, stopping short just before he landed on the garbage bag full of stuff. Jumping over the bag, he raced past the Ping-Pong table, the washer/dryer, and his dad's neatly organized workbench, heading for the big old freezer, half-hidden behind some empty boxes.

The icy packages stung Michael's fingers as he pushed them around, trying to make room for the chili. Digging out a hole between containers of frozen milk and bags of frozen bread, he buried the chili, then covered it with a flat box of frozen pizza. Slamming the freezer top down, Michael raced back across the basement, past the mini-dojo he and his brothers had set up, complete with mirrors, flags, and punching bag.

Michael's next problem was the dirty pots. He had to wash them and put them back in their proper places before his parents noticed they were gone. The problem was, it was almost time for dinner, and Michael had no idea what they were planning to cook. There was a sink in the basement. All Michael needed to do was run back upstairs and grab some dishwashing soap. Then he could come back down, wash the pots, and sneak them back upstairs when his parents weren't around. Maybe he could get Lee or Jeremy to play lookout, just to make sure he wasn't caught.

Hopping over the lumpy garbage bag, Michael climbed up the stairs, his sore legs burning, and raced back into the kitchen. There was a container of liquid soap sitting right on the sink. Just as Michael was reaching for it, he heard his parents heading back down the stairs.

"Maybe if we cover it with a sheet or blanket." Mr. Jenkins was still joking about the table. "Or we could even build a fence around it."

"Stephen!" Mrs. Jenkins warned.

Michael couldn't risk running around the kitchen like a maniac with his parents coming. It would look too suspicious. But he did have time to do two important things. He threw open the window, letting in a blast of fresh winter air that he hoped would suck out the smell of chili. Then he turned on the kitchen fan to help things along. Finally, he rinsed the wooden spoon in scalding hot water.

Michael checked around the kitchen one last time for signs of how he'd spent his afternoon. But there weren't any. Even the smell was almost gone. Of course, there were still the pots downstairs, but that wasn't too major. Michael could take care of them after dinner.

As Michael's parents pushed open the door from the hallway, Michael finally relaxed. He was totally and completely exhausted, but he felt great. He'd proved in one more way that he deserved his new rank of brown belt. He'd done the impossible. And he'd done it without any help from Lee or Jeremy.

Chapter Eight

"You know what I'm in the mood for?" Mrs. Jenkins said as she entered the kitchen. "Mexican food."

"You're always in the mood for Mexican food," Mr. Jenkins said, following her. "We've already had it twice this week."

"Yes, but we haven't had my *favorite* dish . . ."

Michael's heart, which had finally slowed to a normal rate, began to flop around in his chest like a fish. *Don't say it,* Michael silently begged his mother, but of course she couldn't hear him.

". . . Chili!" Mrs. Jenkins's freckled face broke into a smile and her blue eyes sparkled. "Maybe it's the Sloppy Joe you made," she said to Michael, "but I'm inspired. I'll use my mother's famous recipe."

To cook chili for the entire family, his mother would have to use all the dishes Michael had just used.

There was no way Michael could explain why they now lay, jumbled and dirty, in a garbage bag at the base of the cellar stairs. Michael had to do something.

"I hate chili!" Michael cried, even though he knew how ridiculous that sounded. He'd always loved chili and his parents knew it. "I mean, I already ate red meat once today," he stammered, trying to come up with a better excuse. "It's not good to eat too much red meat," he said, his face getting hot. "You have to eat stuff from *all* the food groups, right? I really think I should be eating more fruits and vegetables."

Michael's parents stared at him like he was crazy. No wonder. Then they looked at each other and raised their eyebrows.

"Okay," Mrs. Jenkins said with a shrug. "We'll have vegetable soup. My mother gave us a tub of it to take home the last time we were there. I think she gave us a loaf of her great homemade bread, too."

Michael breathed a sigh of relief. Mrs. Jenkins walked over to the refrigerator and pulled open the lower section, which was the freezer. "Here it is," she said, pulling out a large plastic container.

"I'll make a salad," Mr. Jenkins said. "Michael, call your brothers. It's time to take your stations."

Usually, Michael's dad cooked because he got home from work earlier than their mom. On weekends,

Michael's mom liked to putter around in the kitchen, though she usually just defrosted stuff *her* mother made. Either way, Michael, Lee, and Jeremy had to help. Their dad had posted a duty roster on the refrigerator so that they could keep track of whose turn it was to do which job. You could take the man out of the army, Michael's mom liked to say, but you couldn't take the army out of the man. It showed in things like how Mr. Jenkins organized the chores.

Michael walked to the kitchen door. "Lee! Jeremy!" he yelled up the stairs. "Dinner!"

There was a thundering sound, like a couple of dinosaurs rumbling down the stairs. Lee and Jeremy burst into the kitchen.

"What are we eating?" Jeremy asked, his face flushed. "I'm starving!"

Lee bounded over to the refrigerator to see what his chore for tonight was. Jeremy and Lee certainly looked well-rested and energetic, Michael noted. The two of them had probably spent the afternoon sleeping. Which was what Michael planned to do as soon as dinner was over. No matter how he tried to fight it, his eyes kept closing.

"We're having soup," Mrs. Jenkins said, opening up a low cabinet. Then she knelt in front of the cabinet

and poked her head inside. Michael heard the rattling
of metal. Then her head reappeared above the cabinet door. "That's funny," she said.

"What is?" Mr. Jenkins asked. He was standing by
the sink washing lettuce leaves.

"The big pot," Mrs. Jenkins said. "Don't we keep
it in this cabinet? I need it for the soup."

Michael's eyes flew wide open. He'd forgotten! You
needed a pot for soup the same as you needed a pot
for chili. Now what was he going to do?

Mr. Jenkins turned off the water and bent over to
look inside the cabinet. "Hmmm," he said. "It should
be here."

With his parents' backs turned, Michael dared to
look at Lee and Jeremy. Their panicky expressions
showed they understood what was wrong as well as
he did.

"What did you do with it?" Mrs. Jenkins asked her
husband. "Didn't you just use it the other night to
make spaghetti?"

Mr. Jenkins nodded. "I thought I put it back where
I found it."

Mrs. Jenkins's forehead wrinkled as she frowned at
her husband. "Don't tell me you used it to wash the
Jeep again. I told you to use the bucket in the garage!"

"I swear I didn't do that!" Mr. Jenkins protested. "It was just that one time when the old bucket had a leak. I bought a new bucket."

"Uh huh . . ." Mrs. Jenkins looked like she didn't believe him.

Michael felt terrible. His parents were fighting, and it was all because of him! But he couldn't do anything to stop it, or he'd give himself away.

"Don't yell at each other," Jeremy said. "You've been married for fifteen wonderful years. You should be celebrating, not fighting."

Michael shot Jeremy a look. What was he doing? If he said one more word, he'd give everything away.

"What Jeremy means," Michael said, "is that a pot is so unimportant in the general scheme of things. It's not worth arguing about. *Right,* Jeremy?"

"Uh . . . right!" Jeremy agreed with an embarrassed smile.

"I guess I can heat it in the microwave," Mrs. Jenkins said, standing up. "So, what did you guys do today while we were gone?"

"Nothing you'd be interested in," Jeremy said too quickly.

Michael shot Jeremy another look. Maye it had been a mistake to let Jeremy in on something this important.

Mr. Jenkins, who was now back at the sink with the lettuce, stared suspiciously at Jeremy. "Why don't I believe you?"

Jeremy tried his best to put on an innocent look, but his face was turning red, a sure sign that something was up. That was how Michael could always tell when Jeremy was lying.

"Michael and I took our first official brown-belt class," Lee cut in. "Sensei pushed us really hard, but I loved it. I wish the class could have gone on even longer."

Michael didn't know which was worse. Jeremy nearly spilling the beans, or Lee bragging about how great he did in class. Lee had popped up like a jack-in-the-box after every deep knee bend and had held his Naihanchi squats without moving a muscle. And after it was all over, Lee had had energy to spare. It wasn't fair. Sure, Lee had a higher rank than Michael, but it had been Lee's first brown-belt-only class, too. How come Lee hadn't suffered?

Jeremy took a stack of plates out of the cabinet and walked over to the table, carrying them with his good arm. "Isn't it getting kind of *chilly* in here?" he asked innocently.

Michael glared at his youngest brother. Was Jeremy trying to be clever, or was this another slip of the tongue? "I'll shut the window, okay?" Michael snarled.

"So what should we do now?" Jeremy asked after dinner was over and they'd finished cleaning up the kitchen. Michael had never seen Jeremy get through his chores so fast with both hands, let alone with just one. Maybe he was getting his energy from the three bowls of chocolate ice cream he'd just inhaled.

"Let's go down to the basement and mess around," Lee said. "Maybe we could do some sparring."

"Not you," Mrs. Jenkins called to Jeremy from the sink, where she was washing dishes. "You know what the doctor said. No karate until your hand heals."

"You and I could spar," Lee said to Michael. "I could show you some of the stuff Jamie showed me this afternoon."

Lee was unbelievable. Hadn't he had enough karate for one day? Didn't even one tiny muscle ache anywhere in his entire body? Michael was so exhausted after everything that had happened today that he could have fallen asleep standing up. "I don't know . . ." Michael said, "I'm sort of tired."

"It's okay," Lee said. "I understand."

Was Michael imagining things, or had Lee given him that same sly smile again, the one Michael had been getting from people all afternoon? Michael was getting pretty sick of feeling like a charity case or a pathetic weakling. He'd show Lee he could take the heat.

Michael stood up and pushed his chair back. "You want to spar?" he asked Lee. "Let's go."

A few minutes later, Michael faced Lee in the mini-dojo they'd made in the basement. They stood barefoot on the mat they'd laid over the concrete floor. The cinder-block wall was covered with flags of the United States and Japan, just like in the dojo at the mall. Michael and his brothers had also hung the certificates they'd earned every time they'd been promoted. Lee had the most, of course, including his most recent one, which announced his promotion to black tips. All the certificates were printed on parchment paper and had red and black Japanese letters on them.

"*Kio-tsuke*," Lee called Michael to attention. It was the responsibility of the higher-ranking student to give the commands. Michael drew himself up straight, his hands down at his sides. His heels were touching, and his toes pointed out at a forty-five degree angle.

"*Rei!*" Lee gave the command to bow. Before working with an opponent, you always bowed to show your respect. It didn't matter whether you were in the dojo or in your own basement. It didn't matter whether you were in full uniform or just in sweats and gi shirts like Michael and Lee were wearing now. You always had to show courtesy.

"Onegai-shimasu," Michael and Lee said to each other. They took passive fighting stance, facing each other.

"Wait a minute, wait a minute!" Jeremy said, struggling to boost himself up onto the Ping-Pong table with one hand. "I want a good view. I want to see every single thing you're doing so I'll know more than the other green belts."

Lee dropped his arms for a minute and turned to Jeremy. "You're supposed to learn because you want to improve yourself, not because you want to be better than somebody else."

"Sorry," Jeremy said, settling on the table at last.

"Ready?" Lee asked Michael.

Michael nodded and raised his fists.

"Hajime!" Lee called, meaning "begin."

Keeping his left side turned toward Lee, Michael began to circle slowly around his brother, looking for an opening. The problem was, Lee also had his left side turned toward Michael. That made two major targets, the solar plexus and the groin, hard to reach. Lee's ribs were covered, too, by his bent arms. The only open target was his face.

Since Michael was taller, he had the reach advantage. That meant he could attack Lee while still being too far away for Lee to attack back. And a kick would give him even more of an advantage because his legs were longer than his arms.

Michael raised his left knee high and delivered a front snap kick to Lee's nose. He didn't *land* the kick, of course. Jyu-kumite was just an exercise. You didn't really want to hurt somebody, especially your own brother. The kick wouldn't have landed anyway, because Lee snapped his left arm up in a high block, deflecting Michael's leg and knocking Michael off balance.

Before Michael could lower his left leg, Lee came in with an incredibly low sidesquat punch to Michael's ribs. Though Lee also pulled his punches, even his soft shove sent Michael stumbling backward. Lee was using his smaller size to his own advantage. If you were shorter than your opponent, the important thing was to stay close and stay low, rooted to the ground, so you wouldn't get knocked off balance.

Staying rooted was important no matter what your size. Michael could see that as he struggled to keep from falling. If only he wasn't so tired. His legs felt heavy and numb, like two blocks of lead.

With Lee so low, though, there was something else

Michael could try. He struck at Lee's collarbones with two backfists, a punch where you snapped your wrists, hard, to strike your opponent with the back of your knuckles. A full-power backfist could break a bone.

Again, Michael was too slow to land his techniques. Lee sent Michael's arm flying with a double chest block, then came in close again to land a double punch to Michael's ribs, followed by an elbow to the face. Though Lee's punches didn't hurt, the speed and accuracy of his techniques made Michael feel like a clumsy old dancing bear. Lee was doing karate. What Michael was doing probably looked more at home in the circus.

"Don't forget to block," Lee reminded Michael. "You're leaving yourself wide open."

Okay, so Lee was a much better fighter. That didn't mean Michael was a total idiot. Of course he knew he was supposed to block. He was a brown belt, wasn't he? So what if nobody else believed he deserved it. So what if people were laughing at him for even daring to take the class today. Michael was a brown belt, and he was going to prove it.

Michael refocused his gaze on the base of Lee's neck. That's what you were always supposed to do when facing an opponent. Looking at the neck gave you a sense of your opponent's entire body so you could react quickly, no matter what the attack. If you looked down, you might miss a punch to the face. If you looked at your opponent's face, you might not see a kick coming. But Michael was ready for anything, now.

Lee seemed so calm and confident, so relaxed as he circled Michael. But he had to have a weakness somewhere. There had to be an opening. What could Michael hit?

Then Michael saw it. Totally open and vulnerable. The perfect target. With a last burst of energy, Michael whipped his right leg out to strike at Lee's left knee. Lee moved to block, but Michael was too fast for him. Michael's foot landed precisely, perfectly. Finally! Lee wouldn't be so quick to correct Michael next time.

"Owwwwww!" Lee cried, dropping to the mat and curling into a ball. "Owwwww!" His face was contorted as he wailed.

"What's the matter?" Michael asked, looking down at his brother. "Did I knock you off balance? You know, it's very important to stay rooted."

Lee didn't answer. He just moaned and trembled as he clutched his leg.

Michael was confused. Was Lee so upset about failing to block that he wasn't going to talk to Michael?

That wasn't fair. If you were going to dish it out, you had to be able to take it.

"Hey!" Jeremy said, jumping off the Ping-Pong table and kneeling beside Lee. "What happened?"

Lee's dark brown eyes were shiny with tears as he gazed up at Michael. "I'll tell you what happened," he said, choking a little as he spoke. His voice was so soft Michael could barely hear it. "You just broke my kneecap!"

Chapter Nine

"You're kidding, right?" Michael asked Lee.

Lee's lips were pressed tightly together, and tears leaked out of his tightly closed eyes. The fact that Lee was trying so hard not to show he was in pain made Michael start to worry.

"I'll get Mom and Dad," Jeremy said, dashing from the basement. As he ran, he tripped over the bag of pots but caught himself and barreled up the stairs.

"Let me see," Michael said, bending down. He couldn't believe he'd actually hurt his brother. Michael had barely felt his foot hit Lee.

Lee slowly pulled up the leg of his green sweatpants. "Ahhhh!" he screamed when he saw his bent left knee.

Michael wanted to cry out, too. He'd never seen anything so horrible. Where Lee's knee normally was

was just an indentation, a hollow pocket of skin. But there was a massive lump on the outside part of Lee's leg.

Michael was finding it hard to breathe. He *couldn't* have done this. He'd never hurt anyone. Even when he'd fought Todd Newman at the comic book convention, Todd hadn't been injured. He'd just tripped and fallen, and anyway, Todd had been the one to start the fight. This wasn't like getting a bruise in karate class, either. This was *serious*.

"Lee . . ." he began. "I'm so sorry. . . ."

"What's going on down here?" Mr. Jenkins asked, running down the stairs. Mrs. Jenkins was right behind him, a soapy lather around the edges of her face. She must have been in the middle of washing up for bed when Jeremy found her.

Michael's parents stopped short when they saw Lee's knee, or what was left of it.

"Oh my God," Mrs. Jenkins, her voice dropping about an octave. "I'll call an ambulance."

"No," Mr. Jenkins said. "Let's take him in the Jeep. It'll be faster."

Mr. Jenkins stooped down and slipped his hands under Lee, whose face was now dead white. "I'll try not to jiggle around too much," he told his son. "But it might hurt when I move you."

"Ahhhh!" was Lee's answer as his father lifted him up. His left leg was stuck in a bent position, and his right leg dangled, limp, over his father's arm.

"I'll go warm up the Jeep," Mrs. Jenkins said, running for the stairs. As she did, *she* tripped over the bag of pots.

As Michael followed behind his mother, he kicked the bag out of the way. He didn't want any more of his family getting injured because of him. When he got up to the first floor, he ran for the front hall closet and grabbed Lee's jacket as well as his own. Then he ran for the garage and jumped in the backseat, waiting for his father and brothers.

In less than a minute, Mr. Jenkins was beside Michael in the backseat with Lee laid across his lap. Jeremy rode in the front with Mrs. Jenkins, who drove through the dark suburban streets lit by yellow street lamps.

"You don't have to talk if it hurts too much," Mr. Jenkins told Lee, "but I have to know how this happened."

While Michael waited for Lee to answer, he studied Lee in the yellow light that alternated with darkness. Lee's almond-shaped eyes were shut, and his high cheekbones were slick with tears. His mouth was just a thin line. His body, suddenly, looked very small in

his father's arms. He looked like the little boy Mr.
Jenkins had brought home from the orphanage in
Vietnam seven years ago.

"It was an accident," Lee said, trying to make his
voice sound as normal as possible. "It's not anybody's
fault."

Michael felt a sharp twinge shoot up through his
body. He wanted his parents to believe Lee. Even
more, *Michael* wanted to believe Lee.

"We were sparring," Lee continued, though it was
obviously difficult for him to speak. "Just like we
always do."

"And I accidentally kicked him," Michael volunteered. "I didn't mean to."

"It was my fault, really," Lee added. "I was pushing
him too hard. I forgot Michael just got his brown belt.
I should have gone easier on him."

There it was again. *Michael just got his brown belt.*
Why did it seem that no matter how long Michael
lived, he'd never forget that phrase?

"It looks like Michael should have gone easier on
you," Mr. Jenkins said sternly, turning his head to
look at Michael. Michael sank down a little in his
seat.

Nobody said anything more in the five minutes it
took to reach Midvale Hospital. Mrs. Jenkins sped

into the back entrance that led to the emergency room but brought the Jeep to a gentle stop so she wouldn't jar Lee. "I'll let them know we're here," she said, jerking the gear shift into park and turning off the ignition. Then she jumped out of the Jeep and ran inside. Jeremy jumped out, too, and opened the back door on his side, where Lee and Mr. Jenkins waited.

Seconds later, two men in white raced up pushing a gurney, a kind of stretcher on wheels. Mr. Jenkins slid carefully out of the Jeep and lowered Lee onto the stretcher. Then the two men ran back inside, pushing Lee. Lee screamed out again as the stretcher turned a corner.

"Be careful!" Mrs. Jenkins called to them.

"I'll park," Mr. Jenkins offered. "You go in with the boys and see what needs to be done."

By the time Michael, Jeremy, and their mom had reached the drab beige lobby, Lee was already gone. Michael looked around. All he saw was a vast stretch of gray linoleum, orange plastic molded seats, and a long counter with a clear window that ran along the top. Some of the orange chairs were filled. There was a gray-haired man holding a red-stained kitchen towel to a bloody gash on his forehead. There was a young woman with a streak of hot pink in her short dark hair who clutched her stomach. There was an old man with an aluminum walker in front of him. But there was no Lee.

Mrs. Jenkins ran up to the counter, where a nurse was talking on the phone. "Excuse me." She waved at the nurse. "Excuse me, have you seen my son?"

The nurse, who looked almost as rumpled as her not-so-white uniform, hung up the phone. "Name?" she asked.

"Jenkins," Michael's mother said. "Lee Jenkins. They just brought him in."

The nurse reached below the counter and pulled out a stack of multicolored paper. As she pushed them toward Mrs. Jenkins, Michael saw that they were official forms. "Fill these out," the nurse said.

"But where's my son?" Mrs. Jenkins demanded. "Where have they taken him?"

"Relax," the nurse said. "You're luckier than most. The doctor's already looking at him."

Michael checked his watch. Then he looked up at the clock on the wall. Then he looked down at his watch again. Then he looked up at the clock. Michael had done this so many times in the past hour that his neck was getting sore. But there was nothing else to do.

There was no point watching the door that led farther into the hospital because it never opened. It looked like Lee had been swallowed up, never to return. And Michael didn't want to look at his parents or Jeremy, because every time he did, they looked at him like he was some sort of criminal. It didn't matter what Lee had said on the ride over. It was Michael's fault, and everybody knew it.

"Are you the Jenkins family?"

Michael looked up and saw a young woman holding a clipboard. Her hair was fluffy and shoulder length, with blond streaks, and she wore a white coat over rust-colored pants.

"I'm Dr. Bitterman," she said. "I've just finished examining Lee."

"Is he going to be all right?" Mrs. Jenkins asked, standing up and approaching the doctor. "What happened to his knee?"

"Nothing was broken," she said.

Michael breathed an enormous sigh of relief. He knew he couldn't have hurt Lee that badly.

"But it's still quite serious," Dr. Bitterman continued. "He had a complete dislocation of the patella."

Jeremy gasped. "That's horrible!" Then he looked confused. "What's a patella?"

"It's the kneecap," Dr. Bitterman explained. "If too much force is used against it, it can slide off to the side. That's why Lee's knee looked concave. The kneecap is what gives the knee shape."

"So that big lump on the side of his leg must have been his kneecap," Michael guessed.

"Right," Dr. Bitterman said. "But don't worry. We were able to slide it back to where it belongs."

"So what now?" Mrs. Jenkins asked. "Is that it? Can Lee come home now?"

"Not yet," Dr. Bitterman said. "There's some soft-tissue damage. The tendons around the knee are in pretty bad shape. Lee will have to wear a full-leg cast for a few weeks. They're putting it on him right now."

"Oh, God." Mrs. Jenkins sank back into her chair.

"It could have been a lot worse," the doctor said. "Injuries like this can sometimes cause pieces of bone to break off. Then we'd have to operate. But Lee was lucky, relatively speaking. We did some X-rays and didn't find any fragments."

"I guess we should be happy for something," Mr. Jenkins said.

The door leading into the hospital swung open, and Michael saw Lee being pushed toward them in a wheelchair. His left leg stuck out straight in front of him in a plaster cast. Over his lap were two wooden crutches.

Michael raced the rest of his family to get over to Lee. "How are you feeling?" he asked his brother.

Lee smiled. "Not half as bad as I was before. The worst part was when she slid my kneecap back. I'm just lucky the bone didn't break."

"There's that word again," Mr. Jenkins said. He looked over at Jeremy's cast. "Luck. You weren't any 'luckier' than Jeremy was."

"So when can I take karate again?" Lee asked, looking up at the doctor.

Dr. Bitterman smiled. "You must be pretty serious about it if you're already thinking about going back." Then her expression grew more serious. "I hate to break it to you, but it's going to be at least two months before you can even think about it. You'll have to wear the cast for three weeks, then you'll need five more to rehabilitate the knee. After about five weeks you should be able to walk normally without pain. After that . . ."

"Two months!" Lee wailed. "That's impossible!"

"Just be happy it's nothing permanent," Mrs. Jenkins said. "Is that it, doctor?"

"That's it," Dr. Bitterman said. "I've already made an appointment for Lee to get his cast off, three weeks from tomorrow." She handed Mrs. Jenkins a small

111

white card. "That has the time and the place. You can use the wheelchair to get Lee to your car."

"Thanks," Mrs. Jenkins said, shaking the doctor's hand.

Mr. Jenkins moved around behind Lee's wheelchair. "Thanks for taking such good care of our son."

"Okay," Mr. Jenkins said a few minutes later as he pulled the Jeep out of the hospital parking lot. Mrs. Jenkins also sat in the front, with Jeremy sandwiched between them. Lee sat sideways on the backseat, his left leg extended, and Michael sat next to Lee's left foot. "What *really* happened in the basement? I want the whole story this time, not the one where you cover for each other."

Michael's throat suddenly felt so thick it was difficult to swallow.

"Yeah," Mrs. Jenkins said, turning around to face Michael and Lee. "What were you two trying to do? Kill each other?"

"Of course not!" Michael protested. "We were sparring, just like Lee said."

"These things happen," Lee added quickly. "It's unavoidable."

"No," Mr. Jenkins said, "it's *not* unavoidable."

He made a sharp left turn onto Main Street. They passed the big municipal parking lot and the broad lawn of the town green, where Michael, Lee, and Jeremy had performed in a karate demonstration not too long ago.

"When Lee asked me if he could study karate," Mr. Jenkins said, "I thought it was a good idea. I thought you'd all learn discipline and self-control. I thought it would be good for you."

"It is!" Jeremy said. "I've learned lots of lessons from karate. I'm a lot calmer than I used to be."

"Were you feeling calm when you broke your hand?" Mr. Jenkins asked. "Was that an accident, too?"

Jeremy, who couldn't lie, didn't answer. The whole family knew Jeremy had broken his hand trying to show off.

"Maybe I made a mistake," Mr. Jenkins said. "Instead of helping you find peaceful solutions to problems, I've put weapons in your hands. You just use karate to hurt yourselves and each other."

"It's not true!" Lee started to protest.

"It *is* true," Mr. Jenkins said. "I can't let you keep doing this. I don't think I could live with myself if

113

this ever happened again. Do you realize how lucky you were?"

Michael's heart felt like it stopped short. "What are you saying?" he asked his father. "Are you saying you don't want us to do karate anymore?"

"Let's put it this way," Mr. Jenkins said. "There are plenty of *other* things you can do after school."

Chapter Ten

For a moment, there was no sound in the car but the humming of the motor. It was so peaceful and quiet that Michael could almost believe his whole world hadn't just come to an end. Or maybe this was what the end of the world sounded like.

"You're kidding, right, Dad?" Jeremy asked. "I mean, you wouldn't really ruin our lives that way . . . would you?"

"Let's get straight exactly what I'm doing," Mr. Jenkins said, turning right onto Shaker Hedge Road. "I'm trying to make sure my sons grow up healthy, strong, and with all their arms and legs in working order."

"But Dad . . ." Lee interrupted.

"I know how much karate means to you," Mr.

Jenkins said, "and I know you think I'm being mean. But something's got to give here."

"But not karate," Michael begged his father. "Punish us some other way. Make us stay in our rooms, cut off our allowance, don't let us watch TV anymore."

Mr. Jenkins made a left turn onto Bonny Brook Road, which curved past the Bonny Brook Country Club on their left.

"Dad?" Michael asked. "Aren't you going to say anything?"

"I've said everything I have to say," Mr. Jenkins said. "I don't want to talk about it anymore."

Jeremy turned around and glared over the back of his seat at Michael. "Thanks a lot," he said.

Michael looked over at Lee, who was also glaring. Lee hadn't looked anywhere near this angry when Michael had turned his knee into a crater. Now he looked as if he'd like to chop off *both* of Michael's knees.

There was silence, again, except for the humming motor and the squeaky squelching in Michael's stomach. Michael didn't blame his brothers one bit for being mad at him right now. It was bad enough he'd hurt Lee. But no karate? Michael was sure Lee and Jeremy would never forgive him.

No one said a word for the rest of the ride home.

When they got inside the house, Mr. Jenkins helped Lee up the stairs with his crutches and his cast while Jeremy and Mrs. Jenkins followed close behind. Michael wanted to help, but somehow he felt as if he didn't belong, as if he wasn't wanted. When everyone had disappeared into Lee's room, Michael went into his own room and closed the door.

All Michael had the energy to do right now was change into his pajamas and go to bed. As Michael kicked his shoes into his closet, he noticed his family portrait leaning against the back wall, partially covered by an old flannel shirt. Michael had started it last night.

Pulling the shirt off the portrait so he could look at it, Michael realized he had yet another problem. He'd already sketched a rough outline of his parents, sitting next to each other, with the three brothers standing behind them. The problem was, he'd been planning to draw his brothers and himself wearing their karate uniforms. He'd even designed a special patch for their gi. The patch said "Karate Club," the nickname their father had given them because they were so crazy about karate. Now Michael wasn't sure what to draw. He didn't know whether to put them in their gi or not. He was even tempted to draw himself out of the picture after what he'd done.

"A-hem!"

The sudden sound, coming from directly behind Michael, made him jump. Michael whirled around and saw Jeremy and Lee standing in the center of his room. If Michael hadn't been so tired and depressed, he might have laughed at the sight of them—Jeremy with his hand in a cast and Lee with his cast and crutches. They each looked like Wile E. Coyote after a round with Road Runner.

"Hi," Michael said shyly.

"We've gotta talk," Jeremy said, plopping down on Michael's bed. "This situation calls for serious action."

Lee leaned his crutches against Michael's desk and sat in Michael's desk chair. "Yeah," he agreed. "We've got to make Dad change his mind. I thought two months was a long time to go without karate, but no karate for the rest of my life? I'd have to run away from home and join another dojo under a made-up name."

Michael breathed a little easier. His brothers didn't sound mad at him so much as upset about what their father had done. "I don't think you'll be able to run too far in your present condition," he said to Lee. Covering the portrait with the shirt again, Michael went over to the bed to sit next to Jeremy.

"We've got to get Dad to change his mind!" Jeremy

insisted. "It's not fair for him to cut us off this way. It wasn't karate's fault I broke my hand."

"Yeah," Lee agreed. "Sensei would never have allowed you to break those boards if he'd known. You were just being stupid."

"Stupid?" Jeremy sputtered, blinking rapidly behind his glasses. "Well, what about you? You didn't look too smart when you let Michael land that technique against your knee. Why didn't you block? You're supposed to be an advanced student."

"I'm more advanced than you," Lee said, trying to rise out of his chair.

"Hey, hey!" Michael tried to stop his brothers. "Stop it! We're deshi! We're supposed to have control."

"Control?" Lee demanded, falling back into his chair. His dark eyes glittered angrily. "You have some nerve talking about control after what you did to me."

"I already told you I was sorry," Michael said, "and you know it was an accident. What else do you want me to say?"

"I want you to tell me why you kicked me so hard," Lee said. "You used full power on that kick, maybe more. You know we're supposed to pull our techniques when we spar."

"What are you saying?" Michael asked. "You think I did it on purpose?"

Lee just crossed his arms and looked at Michael. Michael could read the answer in Lee's cold stare.

"What do you take me for?" Michael demanded, jumping off his bed and approaching Lee. "You know, *you're* the one who has a lot of nerve putting the blame on me after everything I did today. Did it ever occur to you that maybe I lost control because I was tired? No, more than tired. Exhausted. And you know why? Because *I* was working all day on Mom and Dad's party while the two of you were goofing off."

"I helped!" Lee insisted. "I chopped the onions and peppers."

"Oh, big deal," Michael said. "Where were you when we were shopping for groceries?"

"I helped, too," Jeremy put in. "I helped you shop for groceries, and I got the recipe from Grandma, and I even threw away your garbage for you after you finished cooking."

"What garbage?" Michael asked. "You were upstairs when I finished cooking."

"The bag in the basement," Jeremy said. "The big black plastic one. I figured you didn't have time to throw it out, so I took care of it."

It took Michael a few seconds to remember the bag

he'd thrown down the stairs, the one people kept tripping over. It took Michael a few more seconds to realize what this meant.

"What do you mean you threw it out?" Michael demanded. "That wasn't garbage! That was pots and pans. Dad and Mom need those to cook with!"

Now it was Jeremy's turn to look blank. "What?" he asked.

"You heard me," Michael practically yelled.

"Well, that wasn't *my* fault," Jeremy said. "It looked like garbage to me. How was I supposed to know what was in there?"

Michael began to pace over his bright red wall-to-wall carpet. "You would have known if you'd been helping me like you were supposed to," he fumed. "But no, you'd rather stay up in your room reading your new *Galaxy Voyagers* book."

"Leave Jeremy alone," Lee jumped in to defend him. "He couldn't have done much anyway with his hand in a cast."

"That's *his* excuse," Michael said, turning back to Lee. "What was yours?"

"Look," Lee said, "we all care about the party. But it's not like we had to get every single thing done today. We still have a week until next Sunday. I don't see what you're getting so bent out of shape about."

121

Why was it that no matter what Michael did or said today, it kept getting twisted around so *he* was the one at fault? "I'm *not* getting bent out of shape!" Michael shouted. "I was just working hard because I care about our parents. Jeremy, at least, had a reason he couldn't help too much, but what about you? You were just being lazy and selfish. You'd rather spar with Jamie Oscarson than do something nice for Mom and Dad."

Lee grabbed his crutches and used them to pull himself up out of his chair. "That's a lie!" he cried, advancing toward Michael. "Take it back right now!"

"I *won't* take it back," Michael said, holding his ground. "I know I'm right, and you know I'm right. You *have* been selfish, and mean, too, making fun of my karate and showing off just because you're more advanced."

"Don't blame me if you couldn't cut it in brown-belt class," Lee said hotly. "That was your fault, not mine."

"We're not talking about me," Michael insisted. "We're talking about the fact that karate matters more to you than your own family."

All the color drained from Lee's face. "Shut up!"

he screamed. "You don't know what matters to me."

"*You* can't face the truth, can you?" Michael goaded. "Well, it's time someone made you face up to it. If you really cared so much about Mom and Dad, you would have pulled your weight this afternoon. I can't believe you'd be so ungrateful after everything they've done for you. But maybe that doesn't matter to you. Maybe you don't really care about them 'cause you're a—"

Michael suddenly clamped his lips together. He couldn't believe what he'd almost said. He'd almost said *adopted*. Maybe Lee didn't really love their parents because he was adopted. Michael had never said, or even thought, such a nasty thing in his entire life. Michael felt mean and ugly inside, like there were slimy worms slithering around in his stomach. What was wrong with him? He felt disgusting.

That was nothing, though, compared with how Michael felt when he saw the look on Lee's face. Lee's mouth was half open, and he was barely breathing. Michael realized with horror that it hadn't mattered that he'd shut his mouth halfway through that . . . word. Lee had known exactly what Michael meant. Jeremy, too, was staring at Michael like he was some sort of monster.

"Lee . . ." Michael started to apologize, but Lee just shook his head. Without a word, Lee planted his crutches a few feet ahead of him and swung forward, aiming for the door. Jeremy didn't so much as look at Michael as he accompanied Lee out of the room and shut the door softly behind them.

Chapter Eleven

The cold wind rushed over Michael's face as he bicycled down the hill to the Midvale Mall. He was heading for the dojo, though he wasn't sure why. He wasn't going to take karate class. He wasn't allowed. So what was he doing here? Michael wondered as he coasted into the mall's vast parking lot. Maybe it was just a Monday afternoon habit.

But, of course, it wasn't a normal Monday afternoon, because Michael was riding by himself. Lee and Jeremy, with their injuries, couldn't have taken karate whether their father allowed them to or not. Lee couldn't even ride a bicycle, and Jeremy wasn't supposed to, so Mrs. Jenkins had driven them to school this morning. There wasn't room for Michael in his mother's tiny sportscar, but it was just as well. Michael knew that the last thing his brothers wanted was to share a small space with him. Come to think of it, the planet Earth was too small for them to share as far as Lee and Jeremy were concerned.

Neither one of them had spoken a single word to Michael since Saturday night. Michael had followed them out of his room and tried to apologize, but the two of them had gone into Lee's bedroom and locked the door. Michael had sat in the hall for half an hour, waiting for them to let him in, but the door had never opened. And all day Sunday, Jeremy had acted like Lee's personal bodyguard, not letting Michael anywhere near him.

Michael's parents had noticed, of course, and had asked what was going on, but no one said a word. Mr. Jenkins thought they were still upset about having to drop out of karate. Not that total silence in the family would make him reconsider. He kept saying that he was more concerned about their safety than anything else and that someday they would understand.

But it was Mr. Jenkins who didn't understand. And Michael was afraid of what would happen if his brothers ever told their father the real reason for their silence. Michael had a feeling that not going to karate would be the least of his problems.

Long before he reached the dojo, Michael spotted the bright red of Sensei Davis's nylon jacket and his black corduroy baseball cap. Sensei was out on the sidewalk in front of the dojo, sweeping. As Michael watched Sensei's calm, relaxed movements, he realized why he'd come. He'd known all along. He'd come to talk to Sensei.

Michael couldn't talk to his parents because then he'd have to explain about the surprise party. And anyway, Sensei was the only person who could help Michael figure out why he had lost control. Sensei was always full of quotes and stories that helped you understand things better. As Michael pulled up to the bicycle rack in front of the dojo, he wondered what Sensei would have to say about this.

Scritch. Scritch. Scritch. Sensei's broom swept up candy wrappers, cigarette butts, and empty paper cups. Michael checked his watch. It was three o'clock. There was still a half hour before the kids' class started. This gave Michael an idea.

"Onegai-shimasu, Sensei," he said, bowing and pulling open the glass door to the dojo. Just his luck, there was a second broom leaning against the wall of the front hallway. Grabbing the broom, Michael dashed back outside and started sweeping as hard as he could.

"Onegai-shimasu," Sensei said. "Did you and your brothers have a nice weekend?"

127

"Oh yes," Michael said, stirring up an enormous cloud of dust and grit. Even if he never got to take karate again, Michael was determined to show brown-belt spirit. That meant doing everything to the best of your ability, even something as simple as sweeping.

Sensei coughed as the wind caught up Michael's dust and scattered it all over the sidewalk.

"Sorry, Sensei," Michael said, trying to push the dust back down to the ground with his broom.

"You have a lot of energy today," Sensei observed. "I hope you'll save some of it for class."

Now it was Michael's turn to cough as some of the dust entered his nose and mouth. Michael fanned the air in front of his face, but he couldn't get a clear breath.

"Okay, okay," Sensei said, patting Michael on the back. "You want some water? Maybe we should go inside."

Michael, who still couldn't breathe, let alone talk, shook his head. "I'm fine," he gasped.

Sensei waited patiently until Michael was breathing normally. Then he started sweeping again.

Michael bit his lip. If he didn't say something soon, all he would have accomplished by coming here was nearly choking to death. "Uh . . . Sensei," he said, "I'm actually not so fine."

Sensei didn't stop sweeping, but he nodded. Michael knew that meant that Sensei was listening and that he should continue.

"This is kind of hard to say," Michael said, sweeping slower, "but this may be the last time you ever see me or my brothers."

"Where are you going?" Sensei asked.

Michael stopped sweeping and leaned on his broom. "I'm not going anywhere," he said. "But it looks like my dad might not let us study karate anymore."

Sensei, too, stopped sweeping and looked at Michael. "Why is that?"

"My dad's mad at us," Michael explained. "Or he's mad at me. Anyway, he's blaming it all on karate even though karate had nothing to do with it. Well, karate had something to do with it, but not the way my father thinks."

Michael knew he was babbling, but Sensei didn't seem to mind. Sensei just gazed steadily at Michael, his dark brown eyes patient and kind. Michael took in a deep breath and tried to clear his mind the way they always did in karate class. Then, slowly and carefully, he told Sensei everything that had happened since Friday, from Jeremy's idea to have a surprise party, to the accident while Michael and Lee

129

were sparring, to the horrible thing Michael had almost said to Lee.

"Even if Lee *was* being selfish by not helping, I had no right to say what I said," Michael concluded. "I think that hurt Lee worse than when I kicked him."

"I think you're right," Sensei said. "Why do you think you said it?"

Michael dropped his eyes, to avoid Sensei's gaze. Then he started sweeping slowly as he tried to come up with an answer. "I have no idea," he said. "I've never said anything like that in my life."

"Do you think it was because you were angry with Lee?"

"Well, I wasn't too happy with him, but I wasn't angry, either. It was more like I went crazy for a minute. I was probably just tired. It was a really long day."

"I'm sure you *were* tired," Sensei agreed, "but why are you so sure you weren't angry?"

Michael looked up at Sensei again. "It's just not my style," he said. "Jeremy's the hothead in the family. I'm more easygoing."

"So you're saying you yelled at Lee because you were tired?"

Michael nodded.

Sensei picked up his broom and headed for the door to the dojo. "Come with me," he said.

Michael quickly swept his pile of dirt over the curb and followed Sensei inside. Sensei leaned his broom against the wall of the front hallway and turned left, heading for the door to his office. He walked around behind the desk, sat down, and pulled out a white index card and a pen.

Michael waited by Sensei's desk. He knew what Sensei was about to do. Sensei was going to write down a quote for Michael to put up on the bulletin board, a quote that would explain this situation. Michael waited impatiently for Sensei to finish, wondering what the quote would say. Maybe it would be something about training harder so you wouldn't get tired so easily.

Or maybe . . . Michael's heart lurched as he thought about it. . . . It would be a quote about how you shouldn't test for a rank until you were really ready. The more Michael thought about it, the more sure he was that this was it. Sensei thought Michael had lost control because he was worn out from brown-belt class.

At last, Sensei finished writing and handed the card to Michael. Michael read it eagerly:

*To make spiritual progress,
you must search for yourself.*

Michael tried to understand the quote, but it just seemed like a bunch of words. "I'm sorry," Michael said honestly. "I don't get it."

"*Everybody* feels anger," Sensei said. "It's part of being human."

"Okay," Michael said, "so maybe I was a little ticked off at Lee, but what does that have to do with the quote?"

"You weren't a little ticked off," Sensei said. "From what you've described, I think you were very, very angry. Furious. And you have every reason to be. Your brothers left you in the lurch, then they ganged up on you and blamed you for what happened. That's why you lashed out."

Michael thought back to the feeling of slimy worms writhing in his stomach and making him do ugly things. This was anger? If it was, Michael wanted to get rid of the feeling as soon as possible. "I'll try not to be angry anymore, Sensei," Michael promised. "Not that it will change anything that's happened."

"No," Sensei said. "You don't understand. You have to accept the fact that you do feel anger. And that you might get angry again. If you don't recognize it, you'll never be able to control it."

Michael sank down into the wooden chair in front of Sensei's desk. Talking to Sensei hadn't cleared things up at all. If anything, he was more confused. All his life, he'd thought of himself a certain way— as a peaceful, calm guy who never wanted to hurt anybody. Now Sensei was telling Michael that he might feel this ugliness over and over again for the rest of his life and that there was nothing he could do about it.

"Look," Sensei said, leaning forward over his desk, "the problem isn't the anger. The problem is not knowing what to do about it. You can't hold it in because the pressure will just build and build until you explode. That's why you lost control when you were sparring."

"Now wait a minute," Michael said. He knew he was being a little bold with Sensei, but he had to defend himself. "I admit I may have felt mad when we were yelling at each other, but the sparring thing was just an accident. I didn't kick Lee hard on purpose."

"It was the same anger," Sensei maintained. "You may not have felt it at the moment, but don't you think it was there?"

Michael dropped his head over the wooden back of the chair. He was starting to understand Sensei's quote. Sensei wanted him to look inside himself and see something he'd never realized was there. But Michael hated what he saw. He felt like a time bomb, ticking, waiting to go off at any moment. "So what am I supposed to do?" Michael asked Sensei. "Lock myself in my room so I don't hurt anybody anymore?"

Sensei rolled back a few inches in his upholstered desk chair. "That would be one solution," he said. "But I think you can find another one."

Michael heard voices in the front hall and turned around. Dwight Vernon and Jon Walker were kicking off their shoes. Alyse Walker, Jon's older sister, was bowing at the entrance to the deck. It was almost time for the kids' class to start. Michael turned back around to face Sensei, who hadn't even changed into his uniform yet. Michael felt bad that he'd taken up so much of Sensei's time, especially since he wasn't sure whether he was even a deshi anymore.

Michael stood up. "I guess I should go," he said. "Thank you for talking to me."

Sensei stood up and bowed. "Arigato," he said. "I hope I see you again."

Michael felt a lump rise in his throat. He couldn't stand the thought of never coming back here, never seeing Sensei or the dojo or any of his friends. If only there were a way to put things right again, to make up with his brothers and make his father change his mind about karate. Karate wasn't about violence and hurting each other. Karate was something that made you stronger, something you could take with you wherever you went. Karate gave you the courage to face up to things.

For the first time in days, Michael smiled. That was it! Even if he never set foot in the dojo again, Michael was still a deshi. That meant he could face up to his problem calmly and bravely. Sensei himself seemed confident that Michael could find a solution. Of course, Michael didn't have any idea what that solution might be, but at least he knew where to start looking—inside himself.

"Arigato, Sensei!" Michael responded, bowing.

Chapter Twelve

"*Commander Johnson, please rise,*" the nasal, strangely accented voice boomed.

Michael, heading toward the front hall from the kitchen, heard the voice coming from the living room. It sounded like it was on television.

"*We the Interplanetary Council find you guilty on all counts,*" the television voice continued. "*You have falsely impersonated a human being when, in fact, you are a Rixian android and a spy!*"

"I knew it!" Jeremy shouted triumphantly. "I told Kevin Whittaker, but he didn't believe me. I should call him up just to shove his face in it."

Michael, entering the living room, nearly collided with Jeremy, who was on his way out. In the white enamel entertainment unit, the twenty-seven-inch color television was tuned to *Galaxy Voyagers*. A man in a green and gold uniform stood behind a futuristic table while a tall blue serpent in gray robes glared down at him.

Jeremy swerved to avoid Michael without so much as looking at him. On the other end of the living room, Lee sat on the turquoise leather sofa, his cast propped up on the matching ottoman. Lee, too, didn't seem to notice that Michael was in the room. Were they going to ignore him forever?

Michael's first instinct was to run upstairs to his room, but he *was* a deshi. He couldn't leave, no matter how scared he was. Michael sent his energy downward, rooting himself to the floor the way he did in kata.

"Wait," he told Jeremy. "We have to talk."

Jeremy kept walking. "We don't have to do anything. Come on, Lee. Let's get out of here. There's suddenly a bad smell in the room."

Michael fought to control his anger. If he lost his cool, he'd never get anywhere with his brothers. He had to stay focused on what he wanted. Michael took a deep breath and backed up a step, blocking Jeremy from leaving.

"I deserved that," Michael said, facing Jeremy. "And you can insult me as much as you want as long as you don't leave the room until I've had my say."

Jeremy merely scowled at Michael. Lee, on the couch, picked up a *People* magazine and started flipping through it as if he hadn't heard.

"I just saw Sensei," Michael began.

"What?" Jeremy interrupted. "You've got to be kidding! First you ruin everything so Lee and I can't do karate. Now you're sneaking around behind Mom and Dad's back. If you think you're in trouble now, wait till they hear about this. I'm telling . . ."

Michael stood patiently, letting Jeremy rant and rave. He tried not to listen too hard to Jeremy's threats. At least one of his brothers was talking to him. That was a step in the right direction. When Jeremy finally ran out of breath, Michael tried again.

"I didn't take karate," Michael explained patiently. "I just wanted some advice from Sensei. I needed to understand what I did wrong."

"You were born," Jeremy snarled.

Ignoring Jeremy, Michael walked over the plush white carpet toward Lee, who was studying an advertisement for laundry detergent as if it were the most fascinating thing he'd ever seen. "Lee," Michael said, looking down at his brother, "I want you to know that I'm very sorry about everything. I never meant to kick you so hard, and I didn't mean what I said."

Lee flipped the page and started reading an article about a TV sitcom actress who had a collection of ceramic pigs.

Michael knew what Lee was doing. While Jeremy was coming on strong in this confrontation, Lee was using a different technique. Lee was fading away, like a shadow. This made it much harder for Michael because you couldn't fight an opponent who wasn't there. But you could try to find him.

"You were absolutely right," Michael said, sitting next to Lee on the couch. "I did lose control. And every word I said was total garbage. The words flew out of my mouth the same way my foot flew out when we were sparring. You're as much my brother as Jeremy is. You're as much a part of this family as any of us, and you always will be." Michael leaned forward so he could try to see Lee's face, but Lee's bangs were blocking his view.

Jeremy approached them and stood over Michael. "Then why'd you ever open your big fat mouth?" he demanded. "What's your problem?"

Michael took a deep breath. "I was mad," he said simply. "Because the two of you stuck me with almost all the work for the party. And I'd gone to a lot of trouble to plan it all so carefully. And because this wasn't the first time you've left me holding the bag."

"What are you talking about?" Jeremy asked. Lee finally looked up from his magazine.

"I've been thinking about this all the way home from the dojo," Michael said, catching Lee's eye, "and I suddenly figured it out. You guys think I'm always gonna be there to pick up the slack whenever you don't feel like doing something. And up till now, you've been right."

"There you go again, always blaming everybody else," Jeremy yelled. "You don't know when to quit, do you?"

"I'm right," Michael insisted. "Remember a few months ago, Jeremy, when you were so busy getting ready for the science fair and the karate demonstration? You waited until the last minute to get started, and I ended up doing all your chores for you, just so you could get everything done on time."

Jeremy started to say something, but then he pressed his lips together. His blue eyes grew thoughtful.

Michael turned to Lee. "And what about the time you took a paper route so you could earn money for that really expensive video game Mom and Dad wouldn't buy you. Remember what happened?"

Lee shook his head.

"You started oversleeping," Michael reminded him. "You would have lost your job if I hadn't taken over your route for you."

"Oh yeah," Lee said quietly.

"Look," Michael said. "I never really minded taking responsibility for you guys. I'm the oldest. It's my job. But I started to really think about it today, and I realized that I've been doing too much for too long. You're not little kids anymore. You're old enough to start pulling your weight."

For a few minutes, no one said anything. On the television, Captain Toltan stripped Commander Johnson of his Starship insignia. Then Lee's mouth twitched in what almost looked like a smile.

"What?" Michael asked.

"I was just thinking about the time I was eight years old," Lee said. "Remember that candy drive for my Little League team? I volunteered to sell two cases of chocolate bars."

"With almonds," Jeremy added, smacking his lips. "I ate a few of those."

"Yeah, but not enough," Lee said. "Two cases was one hundred ninety-two bars of chocolate. And after I'd promised to sell them, I chickened out."

"You were shy," Michael recalled. "And your English wasn't that good yet."

141

"But I was mostly scared," Lee said. "And I was scared to give the chocolate back, because then I'd be letting the team down."

Jeremy sat down on the couch on the other side of Michael. "So Michael sold the candy bars for you."

"Every single one," Lee said, nodding. "I guess you wouldn't have done that for me if you weren't my brother."

Jeremy punched Michael lightly on the shoulder. "I guess he's not a total jerk all the time," Jeremy said to Lee.

Lee shrugged. "I guess not." His brown eyes slid over to look at Michael's face. "And I guess I accept your apology. I'm sorry, too, for not understanding better. I should have realized how much pressure you were under, being hammered by Sensei."

"Huh?" Michael asked. "What are you talking about?"

Lee smiled. "Sensei was 'hammering the nail.' He does that to all new brown belts."

Michael still didn't get it.

"It's a tradition," Lee explained. "When deshi earn their brown belts, they start getting cocky. They think they're hot stuff. So Sensei goes extra hard on them—"

"—to put us back in our places," Michael finished. "Yeah, I guess I was pretty proud of myself."

"You and everybody else," Lee said.

Heaving a deep sigh, Michael leaned back against the smooth leather cushions. "None of this ever would have happened if we hadn't tried to plan this surprise party. Maybe it's just too much. Maybe it's a bad idea."

"Of course it's not a bad idea," Jeremy protested. "I'm the one who thought of it."

"Then I guess I'm the one who screwed it up," Michael said. "And now with you two guys out of commission, we should just forget about it, right? We'll never pull it off now."

"It wasn't just you," Lee said. "We could have helped you more."

"But you were right, too," Michael said. "I didn't have to go so haywire with all my big plans, doing it all ourselves."

"Hey!" Jeremy said. "Why are we talking about the party in the past tense? We still have six days to get ready."

Michael looked from Jeremy, in his arm cast, to Lee in his leg cast. "How are we gonna do that?" he asked Jeremy. "You guys aren't exactly in peak condition."

"We'll ask for help," Jeremy said. "There's nothing wrong with letting Grandma cook something, and Aunt Charlotte keeps asking if she can make her Swedish meatballs."

Michael stared at the TV screen, which showed clips from next week's episode of *Galaxy Voyagers*. It was a rerun, the one where Captain Toltan got caught in a time warp and met himself as a young boy. As the images flashed by, Michael thought about Jeremy's suggestion. Before today, he never would have considered asking for help. But things were starting to look different. Maybe he didn't have to be a superhero and superdeshi and super older brother every minute of every day. He wasn't Turbotron. He was just a kid. And it would be a shame if the party got canceled just because he was stubborn.

"Okay," Michael said. "Let's call Grandma. But *we'll* plan the menu."

Chapter Thirteen

Brrrrring!

Michael had been waiting for the phone to ring for the past half hour. Even so, the sound went through him like a shock wave when it finally came. In fact, he nearly dropped the hot tray of pigs-in-blankets he'd just taken out of the oven.

Brrrrrring!

"Are you going to get that?" Lee asked. He sat at the kitchen table, chopping water chestnuts for Grandma Kussack's famous vegetable dip. It was one of the few things left to prepare for the surprise party, which would be starting any minute. Earlier in the week, while Michael's parents had been out at a movie, Grandma Kussack had pulled up with a carload of everything they'd asked for: lasagna, lemon meringue pie, chicken noodle soup, brownies, fried shrimp, and stuffed olives. Michael had been afraid they'd asked Grandma for too much, but she'd brought a few extra dishes of her own: cabbage soup, a vegetable souffle, and thimble cookies filled with jelly. Michael still wasn't sure how they'd managed to stuff it all in the freezer.

Brrrring!

"Michael!" Lee reminded him. "That's probably Grandma."

"I know, I know!" Michael said, dropping the tray on the stove and taking off his oven mitt so he could answer the phone. "Hello!" he said into the receiver.

"Michael?" It was Grandma. "Your parents just left. They should be home in about fifteen minutes." To get Michael's parents out of the house, Grandma had asked them to come over this morning and help her move some old furniture out of the basement to give to the Salvation Army. She made sure she kept them over two hours, giving Michael and his brothers time to decorate and get all the guests into the house.

"Oh my God!" Michael shouted. "I'd better check and make sure everything's all set up in the dining room. Thanks for everything, Grandma. I'm sorry you won't get here in time for the surprise, but I'll see you soon."

Michael hung up the phone. "They're on their

way," he shouted to Lee as he raced through the swinging door into the dining room.

The room was full of relatives and friends of their parents, all standing around talking and laughing and eating popcorn and potato chips.

"They're on their way!" Michael shouted again. "Everybody, please get in the dining room so I can shut the doors."

Michael threaded through the company to the opposite door leading into the front hallway. He wanted to pick up any stragglers just in case his parents came through the front door. When he reached the hallway, he saw Jeremy standing up on a stepladder, trying to tape up a "Happy Anniversary" sign with his one good hand. Jeremy was trying to balance himself by leaning his cast against the wall, but he didn't look too stable.

"Jeremy!" Michael yelled. "Get down from there! Isn't one broken bone enough?"

"Just trying to hold up my end of the responsibility," Jeremy joked.

"Well, we'll make an exception, just this once," Michael said.

Jeremy climbed down and Michael quickly scaled the ladder to finish taping the sign. "Looks good," he told his brother.

"Hey, guys," said a deep, pleasant voice.

Michael hopped down off the ladder and turned to see Vic Vernon, Dwight's dad, enter from the living room. Vic Vernon was a reporter for the local news station, WMID-TV, and he looked the part. Tall and handsome, with smooth dark brown skin, he wore an expensive gray suit and a heavy gold watch. Dwight's parents were friends with Michael's parents.

"Anything I can do to help?" Vic Vernon asked.

"No, thanks," Michael said, hastily folding up the ladder. "Everything's under control."

Aunt Charlotte and Uncle Herb wandered out into the hall. Aunt Charlotte was Andrea Jenkins's older sister. "What's going on out here?" Aunt Charlotte asked. "Is this where the party is?"

"No, no!" Michael said, opening the dining room door and shooing everyone back inside. "We need to have everyone in the dining room so my parents won't see anybody when they come inside."

A movement on the street caught Michael's eye. Peering through the glass panels on either side of the front door, he recognized his father's Jeep as it shot past the house and pulled up in the driveway.

"They're here!" Michael shouted, practically pushing everyone into the dining room. "Nobody move!"

"Shhhh! Shhhh!" Aunt Charlotte went around to the guests, quieting them down. "They're here!"

Michael dashed through the dining room, back into the kitchen, where Lee had already removed all traces of the vegetable dip. The only sign of a party was the chili, simmering on the stove in a new pot Michael's parents had just bought. Michael ran for the chili. He wasn't going to let it trip him up again. Quickly dumping the chili into a big bowl, Michael carried it into the dining room, where Mrs. Vernon took it from him. Then he ran back to the kitchen, where Lee and Jeremy had already taken their posts.

Jeremy had had another great idea. He'd decided that all three of them should be sitting eating cereal in the kitchen when their parents walked in. They'd pretend they'd just woken up, then Michael would tell his parents a package had arrived while they were out and that it was in the dining room.

The garage door rumbled as it opened. Michael plunked down in his usual place. Jeremy had already poured the milk in everyone's cereal, and there were three glasses of orange juice on the table.

"Look natural," Lee advised them as they started spooning up the cereal.

Jeremy ran his hands through his hair to make it messy. "So it looks like I just woke up," he explained.

Michael heard the Jeep pull into the garage and

the engine shut off. Then he heard footsteps. The doorknob to the kitchen door turned.

"We're home!" Mrs. Jenkins called as she entered the kitchen.

Jeremy immediately started grinning, and his face turned bright red. Michael kicked Jeremy under the table. After all they'd been through, he didn't want Jeremy to give away the surprise with the goofy expression on his face. Jeremy quickly stuffed a spoonful of cereal in his mouth and covered the lower half of his face with a napkin.

"How's the neighborhood branch of Midvale Hospital doing?" Mr. Jenkins asked, following his wife into the kitchen. "No new injuries, I hope."

Lee jumped up, despite the cast on his leg. "Of course not!" he practically shouted. "My knee's feeling much better. You know, I think all my karate training's helped me heal faster."

Michael would have kicked Lee under the table, too, if Lee hadn't been wearing a cast. Lee was starting to give away the other surprise, the one they were planning to spring on their parents *after* the party.

Michael cleared his throat and glanced from Lee to Jeremy. "How's Grandma?" he asked, trying to sound casual.

"She's fine," Mr. Jenkins said, closing the garage door behind him. "She sends you her love."

"So?" Mrs. Jenkins asked, heading for the refrigerator. "Anything exciting happen while we were gone?"

Michael suddenly remembered that there were about a dozen bottles of soda in the refrigerator. They'd give away the party for sure. "Uh, Mom!" Michael yelled, leaping from his chair and darting between his mother and the refrigerator. He stood panting with his back against the refrigerator door. "Actually, something exciting *did* happen. You got a package."

"Oh?" Mrs. Jenkins tried to find a way around Michael, but he held his ground. "Excuse me," she said. "I want to get some orange juice."

"I'll get it," Michael said, opening the refrigerator door just wide enough to grab the container.

"Thank you," Mrs. Jenkins said. "So? What kind of package?"

"Why don't you see for yourself?" Michael asked. "It's in the dining room."

Mrs. Jenkins took a glass out of a high cabinet. "Okay," she said. "I just need to make a phone call first."

After pouring some juice, Mrs. Jenkins headed for the phone. She seemed to be moving incredibly slowly. Michael had to make something up, quick.

"Actually," Michael said, "you might not want to wait. The package was marked . . . urgent."

"Really?" Mrs. Jenkins put her juice glass down on the table. Then she headed for the dining room door.

"You'd better go too, Dad," Michael prompted his father. "The package was addressed to both of you."

Mr. and Mrs. Jenkins headed for the dining room door. Lee grabbed his crutches and followed them, with Michael and Jeremy right behind. Michael held his breath as Mrs. Jenkins pushed open the door.

"Happy Anniversary!" shouted a sea of happy faces as flashbulbs popped. Michael recognized Tony Newman, his mom's former boss from another comic book company; his dad's cousin Janet, who'd flown all the way in from California; some of the illustrators from Rocket Comics; Harry and Marjorie Boerger, their next door neighbors . . . and Grandma Kussack! Michael was amazed. How had she gotten here so fast? She'd left her house after his mom and dad did.

Mr. and Mrs. Jenkins walked slowly into the dining room, stunned looks on their faces as everyone surrounded them. "I can't believe it!" Mr. Jenkins was saying. "Where did you all come from?"

Michael suddenly felt free and light. All the planning had paid off. No matter what else happened, the party would be a success. There was just one thing Michael had to find out.

"Grandma," he said, pulling Grandma Kussack away from his parents. She was petite and pretty, like his mother, but her curly hair was short and white.

"Hi, sweetness," she said, planting multiple kisses on his cheek. "We did it, huh?"

"Yeah," Michael said. "But tell me something. How did you get here in time for the surprise?"

Grandma smiled. "Well, I might have broken the speed limit just a little bit."

Chapter Fourteen

"Look at your face in this one, Stephen!" Mrs. Jenkins teased later that evening as she went through a stack of snapshots from the party. "Your mouth is open so wide you could drive a train through it."

The whole family sat together in the living room, Mr. and Mrs. Jenkins and Lee on the couch, Michael and Jeremy on the floor beneath them.

Jeremy took the photograph from his mother. "You do look pretty shocked, Dad," he agreed. "I guess that means you were really surprised, right?"

Michael laughed. This had to be the fiftieth time Jeremy had asked that question. No matter how many times their parents assured them that yes, indeed, they really had been completely surprised, Jeremy kept asking.

"The thing that amazes me," Mr. Jenkins said, "was

how you guys could pull off such a major event. You must have been planning this for weeks."

"We're deshi—" Jeremy started to say, but Michael gave him a look. As the great samurai warrior Musashi used to say, there is timing in everything. If Lee and Jeremy kept jumping the gun like this, they'd mess up the second surprise.

"Well," Michael's mom said, leaning back against Michael's dad, "this was the best anniversary we've ever had."

This was Michael's big cue. *Now* it was time for Anniversary Day—Part Two. "It's not over yet," Michael said, jumping up off the rug. "I'll be right back." Michael ran upstairs to his room and grabbed a square flat object wrapped in silver paper. He raced back down to the living room.

"Another present?" Mrs. Jenkins asked disbelievingly. "We can't take this. You boys have done enough already."

"You have to take this," Michael insisted, placing the package on his mother's lap. "I want you to." *You don't know how much,* he added to himself.

"Help me open it, Stephen," Mrs. Jenkins said to Mr. Jenkins.

The two of them ripped open the package, and their eyes opened wide when they saw Michael's family portrait. Jeremy and Lee, too, craned their necks to see. Michael hadn't shown it to anyone. He hadn't even finished painting it until late last night. But now it looked exactly the way he wanted it to. The question was—what would his parents think?

"It's . . . very nice," Mrs. Jenkins said, staring down at the picture. Mr. Jenkins said nothing.

Michael knew why they were less than enthusiastic. Michael had drawn his brothers and himself in their karate uniforms. Now that Michael had gotten his parents thinking, it was Lee's turn to make his pitch. Michael nodded silently at Lee.

"I know you're probably wondering why we're wearing our uniforms in the picture," Lee began, "and Michael didn't mean to be disobedient or disrespectful or anything like that. You're our parents, and we have to listen to you. But we want you to know how important karate is to all of us. We can't give it up just because of a few injuries. Karate is my life!"

"And it's made us really strong," Jeremy cut in, flexing his good arm to show off his biceps.

Michael glared at Jeremy. This wasn't the way they'd rehearsed it.

Jeremy blushed. "I meant, it's made us strong *mentally*. Like, remember the time I fell down at the karate demonstration in front of everyone? Sure, I was totally embarrassed, but I learned a lot from that. I learned not to try to do too many things at once."

Michael looked at his parents to see how they were taking this so far. Mr. Jenkins had his arms crossed over his chest and Mrs. Jenkins was frowning. Not a good sign. But Michael had more up his sleeve.

"And remember the time the Whittaker kids were picking on Lee?" he asked. "Karate helped us realize you have to get to know your enemy and win without fighting."

Mr. Jenkins smiled and shook his head. "As I recall," he said, "there *was* a fight. Several, in fact. Jeremy got his glasses broken and a fat lip, then Lee fought with Jason. Correct me if I'm wrong."

Michael thought hard. His father was right, of course, but that wasn't the whole story. "We didn't go looking for a fight," Michael said. "We did everything we could to prevent it. But sometimes fights come looking for you."

"And it ended okay," Lee added. "We *did* get to know Jason, and we're almost friends with him now."

Mrs. Jenkins laughed and put the portrait beside her on the couch. "I think I'm beginning to understand," she said. "This surprise party was just to butter us up, right? So we'd change our minds about karate?"

"No!" Jeremy exclaimed, banging his good fist on

the couch. "Most of our problems started *because* of the party."

Michael gave Jeremy another look to shut him up. The last thing any of the brothers wanted was to make his parents feel bad about the party.

Jeremy nodded to show he'd understood. "What I meant was—we gave you the party because we love you. It had nothing to do with karate. But our injuries had nothing to do with karate, either. I broke my hand because I was showing off. I wasn't even supposed to be breaking boards."

"And if I'd been using karate correctly," Michael added, "I never would have hurt Lee. Karate's supposed to teach us to control our anger. But I couldn't control it because I didn't even know I *was* angry."

"What were you angry about?" Mr. Jenkins asked.

Michael couldn't tell his parents that Lee and Jeremy hadn't done much to help prepare for the party. He'd sound like he was trying to take all the credit himself. And, anyway, it wasn't true anymore. Jeremy and Lee had really come through in the end.

"Let's put it this way," Michael said. "Karate's made me see a lot of things inside myself I never knew were there. I don't like everything I see, but at least I can try to deal with them."

Mr. Jenkins screwed up his mouth and wrinkled

his forehead. Mrs. Jenkins's blue eyes grew dreamy as she stared at nothing. Michael tried not to get too hopeful, but it looked like his parents were at least reconsidering. Then Mrs. Jenkins's eyes snapped back into focus.

"I don't know," she said. "I hear what you're saying, and I believe you, but I don't want to spend the rest of my life driving you to doctors and emergency rooms."

"And *I* worry that your fists are developing faster than your minds," Mr. Jenkins said. "I'm glad you're learning all these important lessons, but I don't want you to kill each other while you're learning them."

"Please, Dad," Jeremy begged. "Just give us one more chance. If you do, we promise we'll never lose control again."

Michael put his hand out to touch Jeremy's arm. "No," he said. "It's unrealistic to think we'll be perfect in the future. After all, we're just *human beings*. We're bound to make mistakes. But at least karate gives us a way to understand our mistakes and learn from them."

"And not make those same mistakes again," Lee said.

Mr. Jenkins gave a deep sigh as he looked from Michael to Lee to Jeremy and back to Michael again.

"You guys don't give up, do you? You learn that in karate, too?"

Michael nodded.

"Maybe we should send them to law school," Mrs. Jenkins said. "They could argue cases together. I'd just hate to be on the other side."

Michael tried not to smile. He knew they were getting somewhere. "So?" he asked. "What do you think? Can we take karate again?"

Mr. Jenkins put his arm around his wife. "Excuse us," he said. "I need to confer with my colleague." He whispered something in her ear and she nodded. Then she whispered something back.

Michael looked at his brothers. Lee was biting his lower lip, and Jeremy kept pushing his glasses up his nose, even though they weren't falling down. Michael tried to clear his mind so he wouldn't be nervous while his parents were making up their minds, but this was one time when karate didn't work. His mind kept filling with the same words, over and over again. *Please say yes, please say yes, please say yes.*

At last, Mr. and Mrs. Jenkins stopped whispering. Michael's father cleared his throat. He looked very serious. So serious that Michael was beginning to worry about his answer.

"One more chance," Mr. Jenkins said quietly.

Michael and his brothers cheered at the top of their lungs.

"Whoooooooooo!" Michael whooped, pumping his fist in the air. He couldn't wait until tomorrow to see Sensei Davis and tell him they were coming back. It had only been a week since he'd been to the dojo, but it felt more like a year.

Michael raised his right hand to give Jeremy a high five but stopped when he saw Jeremy's cast. Switching to his left hand, Michael patted Jeremy lightly on the shoulder. Michael wanted to slap Lee on the back, but he didn't want to jar Lee's leg, which was also encased in plaster.

Michael took a deep breath to calm himself. Happy as he was, he couldn't forget what his father had said. No matter how much karate had helped him in his life, it was still a dangerous weapon. You had to respect it as much for the harm it could do as for the good.

Know thyself, and you will know the universe.
                    —Socrates

Glossary

Arigato—Thank you

Bo—Weapon. Wooden staff with tapered ends

Cat stance—Body weight rests on the bent back leg. Front foot lightly touches the floor. Most advantageous for attacking an opponent's side

Deshi—Karate student (below black-belt level)

Dojo—Sacred hall of learning. Karate school

Down block—Downward strike with forearm, used against attack aimed at lower body

Fukyugata Ichi—First white-belt kata composed of walking and reverse punches, down blocks and high blocks. Most basic kata

Gi—Karate uniform

Hajime—Begin

Jyu-kumite—Freestyle sparring

Karate—Weaponless form of self-defense. Literally means "empty (kara) hand (te)"

Karate ni sente nashi—There is no first attack in karate

Kata—Form. An organized series of pre-arranged defensive and offensive movements symbolizing an imaginary fight between several opponents and performed in a geometrical pattern. Handed down and perfected by masters of a system of karate

Kiai—Concentration of energy and power in one sharp burst, sometimes accompanied by a loud shout used to startle opponent

Kio-tsuke—Attention

Knife hands—Four fingers straight and pressed stiffly together. Thumb pressed in tightly. Side of hand used to slash or strike an opponent

Ma-ai—Sense of proper distance from an opponent

Naihanchi—A rooted, squatting stance with heels turned out and toes turned in

Naihanchi Sho—First brown-belt kata. Features wide-legged "horse" stance. Trains lower parts of the body

Nunchuku—Weapon. Flail. Two wooden sticks connected by a rope

Onegai-shimasu—Please teach me

Promotion—Test for next rank, in which student performs kata and other techniques for a board of black-belt judges

Rei—Bow

Sai—Weapon. Slender pointed weapon resembling sword

Samurai—Japanese warrior

Sempai—Senior student

Sensei—Teacher or master

Shinden—Old masters, teachers who came before us

Solar plexus—Nerve center located beneath the rib cage. A vulnerable target

Te—Hand

Yame—Stop

Yo-i—Ready

COUNTING

Ichi—One
Ni—Two
San—Three
Shi—Four
Go—Five
Roku—Six
Shichi—Seven
Hachi—Eight
Ku—Nine
Ju—Ten

Carin Greenberg Baker has written many books for young readers but claims the Karate Club series is her favorite. "I'm a deshi, too," she says, "and writing about karate is another way to help me learn more." She has studied karate for several years at the dojo owned by her husband, Sensei David Baker, and recently earned the rank of green belt with brown tips. When she's not practicing karate or writing about it, she serves as the co-headwriter of *Ghostwriter*, a weekly television series on PBS.